SUPER SiSTER
and the
Birthday Party

Gwyneth Rees is half Welsh and half English and grew up in Scotland. She went to Glasgow University and qualified as a doctor in 1990. She is a child and adolescent psychiatrist but has now stopped practising so that she can write full-time. She is the author of many bestselling books, including the Fairies series, the Cosmo series and the Marietta's Magic Dress Shop series, as well as several books for older readers. She lives near London with her husband, Robert, and their daughters, Eliza and Lottie.

Visit www.gwynethrees.com

Gwyneth Rees

SUPER SISTER
and the Birthday Party

Illustrated by Ella Okstad

MACMILLAN CHILDREN'S BOOKS

First published 2013 by Macmillan Children's Books
a division of Macmillan Publishers Limited
20 New Wharf Road, London N1 9RR
Basingstoke and Oxford
Associated companies throughout the world
www.panmacmillan.com

ISBN 978-0-330-46142-9

1 3 5 7 9 8 6 4 2

A CIP catalogue record for this book is available from
the British Library.

Printed and bound by CPI Group (UK) Ltd, Croydon CR0 4YY

In memory of Harold Dawson –
my very wonderful grandad

MEET THE

EMMA

SAFFIE

MUM

DAD

DOROTHY & ELVIRA
Saffie's dolls

CHARACTERS

GRANNY

GRANDPA

HOWARD

CEDRIC

QUEENIE-MAY

It's not as easy as you might think being
a nine-year-old girl with a superpower!
It's especially not easy when you have
a mischievous little sister with the *same*
superpower, who *you're* supposed to keep
out of trouble!

My name is Emma and I live with my
two ordinary parents, Marsha and Jim, and
my six-year-old sister, Saffie. My sister
and I were born with a very special gift.
It's not that we can fly, or make ourselves
invisible, or read minds, or make our bodies

incredibly elastic or anything like that. But
what we *can* do is make all sorts of non-
living things come to life – which Mum
says is called *animation*. Think toys, pencils,
plants, brooms, cutlery, shoes, broccoli
and garden gnomes all dancing around and
talking to each other and you'll get the idea.

This weird gift runs through my mum's side of the family and, according to Granny, it came about when one of our ancient ancestors got struck by lightning. Apparently some of their normal DNA got mutated into super DNA or something. Of course, we don't really know if that's true, but what we *do* know is that the family gift always skips a generation, which is why it missed out Mum and jumped straight from Granny to us. (Mum has always been perfectly normal – though she says she doesn't *feel* normal having us around.)

Having superpowers can be a lot of fun. Saffie and I can make our dolls and teddy bears *really* talk to us – not just pretend talking – and it's pretty cool getting to play frisbee with Granny's garden gnomes! But the downside is that we have to keep our superpowers a secret because Mum is scared that if anyone finds out about us we'll never be able to lead normal lives ever again.

I've always been very cautious when it comes to using my power, but Saffie isn't careful in the least and it can be really hard work keeping her out of trouble. That's why there are times when I honestly feel like I deserve a *medal* for being her big sister – like last summer, when we were sent to stay with Granny and Grandpa for the holidays . . .

CHAPTER 1

It was first thing in the morning on the day my sister and I were going to Granny and Grandpa's house for the summer holidays. I was pretty excited. This was going to be the first time we'd stayed there without our parents. Mum, however, was starting to get super-stressed.

'Where's Saffie?' she asked as she watched me stuff some last-minute things into my travel bag in the hall.

'Upstairs saying goodbye to her dolls,' I said. Seeing the panic on Mum's face I added quickly, 'Don't worry, Mum. She's only saying goodbye to them in a *normal* way.'

Mum looked relieved until Dad ruined it by grunting, 'That child couldn't do anything normal if she tried.'

'Jim, would you please stop encouraging the girls to think they're not *normal*!' Mum snapped. 'I know this is harder for you because you didn't grow up in a family with all this . . . this . . .'

'*Weirdness?*' Dad supplied for her.

'. . . this *extraordinary* behaviour taking place,' Mum continued, scowling at him. 'But despite that, you ought to know by now that Emma and Saffie are two perfectly normal children who need us to treat them that way.'

Normalness is a topic that comes up a lot

in relation to Saffie and me. I'm sure that if you met us you'd probably think we were both perfectly normal – or at least you'd think that until you got to know us a bit better . . .

'Granny says that normal is just another word for *boring*,' I informed them.

'*She would.*' Mum was looking even more worried. 'Oh dear . . . I hope I'm doing the right thing sending you two girls to stay with her for the holidays.'

'We haven't really got much choice, Marsha,' Dad reminded her gently.

Keeping our superpowers a secret has always been difficult, but it had become ten times harder last summer. You see, at the start of the holidays our next-door neighbours had moved out and new ones had moved in –

and the new ones turned out to be really nosy and super-interested in us. Mum was terrified they'd find out the truth, so Granny had come to stay with us to try and help. But that had only made things worse, so Granny then suggested that Saffie and I went to stay with *her* for the summer instead.

'I can drive home tomorrow and get things ready, and you and Jim can bring the girls at the weekend. At least that will get them away from your neighbours for a while. And when they're with me I can teach Saffie how to control her superpower a bit better. She's a bright girl. I'm sure she'll learn quickly.' She paused. 'And I can teach Emma a few things too.'

'*What* things, Granny?' I had asked her in surprise.

'Just you wait and see,' Granny had

replied, giving me one of her winks.

But later I'd heard Mum and Granny talking about me when they thought I was asleep in bed.

'Don't push Emma too hard,' Mum was saying as I listened from the top of the stairs. 'Emma's power is much weaker than Saffie's. She's quite sensitive about it, though she'd never say so.'

I'd felt a bit uncomfortable hearing Mum say that. We don't normally talk about the difference in our superpowers – the fact that I can only make small things come to life whereas Saffie can animate massive objects if she wants to. The previous week she'd brought to life both our next-door neighbours' garden shed *and* a dustbin lorry.

'The trouble with Emma is that she doesn't use her power enough,' Granny was saying. 'Use it or lose it, that's what she needs to understand.'

'The less she uses it the better, as far as I'm concerned,' Mum said with feeling.

'That's because you're only concerned with keeping the girls safe,' Granny replied. 'But the more skilled they are at using their powers, the safer they'll be in the long term. They have their whole lives ahead of them, remember. It's no use you protecting them too much or they'll never learn how to take care of themselves . . .'

'Mother, they're only children. They need protection. And if you don't agree with that then—'

'Of course I agree,' Granny cut in impatiently. 'I'm just saying there's a difference between protection and *over*protection, that's all.'

After that they changed the subject, but the next morning Mum seemed a bit more reluctant to let us go to Granny's.

'Are you sure you'll be all right having them with you for all that time, Mother? Jim and I can come at the weekends, but I really think it might be better if I stayed during the week too.'

But Granny had been adamant that she didn't think that was a good idea. 'The last thing Saffie needs while I'm teaching her how to control her superpower is you fussing over her. If you just relax and leave things to me she might even be ready to go to school with Emma by the end of the holidays.'

Mum let out a surprised gasp. 'Mother, do you really think so?'

And that had settled it, because if there's one thing guaranteed to make Mum agree to anything, it's the prospect of not having to homeschool my little sister any longer.

'Speaking of Granny, don't we have to get going soon?' Dad said. 'She wanted us there in time for lunch, didn't she?' It was Sunday and Granny was making a roast dinner.

'LOOK OUT!' yelled a high-pitched voice and we looked up to see Saffie hurtling down the banister rail towards us. She was dressed in a yellow long-sleeved leotard with a silver star on the front, a shiny red cape, a pair of stripy tights and her silver wellington boots. Her curly reddish-brown hair looked like it hadn't been brushed in a week and she still had jam on her face from breakfast.

'Oh, Saffie,' Mum sighed as my little sister landed on her feet with a thump and flicked her red cape out of the way as she spun round to face us. 'You wear that Supergirl outfit all the time. Why can't you wear that pretty princess costume you got for your birthday?'

Saffie scowled. 'I don't like it. It makes me look like a . . . a . . .'

'Princess?' Dad suggested with a smile.

Saffie nodded. 'Like a silly old princess

that needs rescuing and I'm *not*!' She stamped her foot to emphasize the last word.

We all laughed and Mum said, 'I suppose you've got a point there. Come on. Time to get going. Oh, and we might as well take Grandpa's birthday present with us so that Granny can check it's the right thing. I can't believe he's going to be seventy on Friday.'

Saffie looked excited. 'Will he have a birthday party? And a cake with seventy candles on it? And balloons . . . and a grown-up pass the parcel like we had on Daddy's birthday, and—'

'Somehow,' Dad interrupted drily, 'I can't imagine your grandpa going for that idea.'

Dad was right. Grandpa isn't really a party person. Whenever we go there he's nearly always out on his allotment, or shut away in his garage workshop making models. And even if he *is* inside the house he's usually stuck behind his newspaper completely oblivious to everything that's going on around him.

'I bet *I* can get him to have a birthday party,' Saffie declared.

She had a certain look on her face, the look she gets when she's determined to make something happen regardless of whether anyone else wants it to or not.

'I don't think so, dear,' Mum said. 'Grandpa can be even more stubborn than you about some things – and avoiding parties is definitely one of them.'

But Saffie was already distracted by the large box wrapped in birthday paper, which Dad was carrying into the hall. 'Ooh, is that his present? What is it?' she asked excitedly.

'Wait and see,' Mum said firmly. 'This is a

15

very special present from us *and* Granny, so we have to take extremely good care of it.'

'Does Grandpa know what it is?' I asked curiously.

'No, it's going to be a big surprise – and I don't want you girls to utter a word about it,' Mum told us firmly.

'Saffie, you can't *make* someone have a birthday party if they don't want one,' I told her as we headed out to the car.

I was taking care not to look in the direction of Mr Seaton, our neighbour, who was outside in bright red shorts and a T-shirt, mowing his front lawn. It hadn't taken us long to find out that Mr Seaton worked in television, that he had a chat show called *Freaky Families on the Sofa* and that we would be just the type of family he would *love* to

16

sniff out. To make matters worse, his wife was a scientist who specialized in studying inherited abnormalities in humans.

I was carrying Howard, the teddy bear I was taking with me to Granny's. Howard has always been extremely sensible when he comes to life – unlike Saffie's dolls.

Saffie was carrying her china doll Elvira in one hand, her frisbee under her other arm and her spotty rucksack packed with stuff for the journey on her back.

'What's that?' I asked as I saw some strands of red woollen hair poking out the top of the rucksack. 'Saffie, you haven't brought Dorothy as well, have you? You know Mum said you could only bring one doll.'

Saffie's doll-animating had been getting a bit out of hand recently as her two favourite dolls, Elvira and Dorothy, were always

fighting. Sometimes it could get quite nasty, like the day before, when they had been hurling marbles at each other.

Saffie gave me her scowliest look. 'I *can't* leave Dorothy behind! She'll be too upset.'

'She *can't* get upset if you haven't brought her to life,' I pointed out. 'Dolls don't usually *have* feelings, remember . . .'

Saffie looked at me as if she thought I was being incredibly stupid. 'What I *mean* is that she'll be upset when I come home and bring her to life and she finds out I took Elvira with me and not her!'

'Oh . . .' I had to admit she had a point. Dorothy and Elvira can get *extremely* jealous of each other if they think my sister isn't treating them fairly.

I decided not to say anything to Mum, because I didn't want to set off one of Saffie's big strops. Besides, since I was going to Granny's too I reckoned I'd be able to keep an eye on both dolls.

'Just look at that,' Mum said, glaring at our neighbour as she and Dad climbed into the car a few minutes later. 'Look at the way he's staring at us . . . and look up there . . .' She was pointing to an upstairs window, where Mrs Seaton was standing with the curtains pulled back and a pair of binoculars trained on us. The Seatons had seen a few odd things since they'd moved in, and after Granny had come to visit (with all her garden gnomes) they had become even more suspicious. Mr Seaton had actually seen Granny's gnomes playing frisbee with Saffie in the garden and we'd had a really hard time explaining that away.

'What does she think she's doing? Looking at animals in a zoo?' Mum complained with a scowl.

'Freaky families in their natural habitat more likely,' Dad joked, which made Saffie and me laugh.

But Mum wasn't laughing. She was fuming as she said firmly, 'The sooner we get the girls away from here the better!'

CHAPTER 2

'OK, girls, not far now,' Dad announced two hours later as we drove past the garden centre on the main road that leads into our grandparents' village.

'One thing I've never understood,' Dad said to Mum, 'is why your father needs to grow vegetables on an allotment when they have such a large garden.'

'Oh, well . . . that's because Dad doesn't feel like he can *do* anything in the garden without asking Walter first,' Mum said.

'Walter?' Dad looked mystified.

'Granny's Head Gnome,' Saffie piped up. 'He's in charge of all the others, plus he's the Head Gardener as well. He always calls me "Miss Serafina". He says everyone should call me by my proper name because it's so pretty.'

'Yes, and he calls me "Miss Emmeline", even though I keep telling him I *hate* my proper name,' I put in grumpily.

'Emma thinks her real name makes her sound like someone's smelly old great-aunt,' Saffie piped up with a giggle.

'Not smelly, just *old*,' I corrected her, because Saffie always exaggerates.

'Walter was my mother's very first garden gnome,' Mum was explaining to Dad as he started to look out for Granny's street, 'and she treats him a bit like he's her Number One Son. I'm afraid he's a bit of a bossy boots with all the others, isn't he, girls?'

Saffie and I both nodded.

Dad was turning the car into the quiet road where our grandparents live on the edge of the village. Their garden backs on to a small field and then some woods.

'Oh . . . my . . .' Dad started to laugh as we drew up outside the house. 'Looks like somebody's got a new hobby!'

Granny and Grandpa's perfectly ordinary – if rather high – front hedge had been transformed into a display of different bird shapes. There was a duck, a peacock, a swan and a seagull with spread-out wings, all perfectly trimmed.

'Wow!' Saffie exclaimed. 'How did they make it grow like that?'

'They cut those shapes into the hedge, Saffie – it's what's known as topiary,' Mum explained.

Granny flung open the front door as we all climbed out of the car. Granny is quite tall, and plump in the middle, with thick hair that is almost as curly as Saffie's. She has green almond-shaped eyes, which Dad says remind him of a cat's, and she has round glasses that are always slipping down her nose.

'My goodness, Saffie – you're not *still*

wearing that Supergirl costume, are you?'
she exclaimed as she came down the path to
greet us.

'She's been wearing it every day this
week,' I said. 'She won't even let Mum put
it in the wash, will she, Mum?'

Mum didn't answer me. Instead she
pointed at the front hedge. '*Please* tell me
the gnomes didn't do this, Mother.'

'Of course they did it,' Granny said. 'Aren't they clever?'

'But what if one of your neighbours saw them?'

'Oh, I doubt that,' Granny said breezily. 'Walter and his team completed the whole thing under cover of darkness . . . using their night-vision goggles of course.'

'*Night-vision* goggles?' Dad was gaping at her. 'You're not serious, Harriet?'

'She is, I'm afraid,' a second elderly voice broke in, and we looked across to see Grandpa standing at the side door of the garage, smiling at us. Grandpa is tall and quite thin with a round face and dark brown eyes. A long time ago he used to have very dark hair too – we've seen it in photos – but for as long as I can remember he's been almost bald. He was wearing his

26

blue workman's
overalls and
wiping his hands
on a paint-
stained cloth.
I guessed he
must be in
the middle of
working on one
of his models.

'Hi, Grandpa!' Saffie and I both called
out as Mum smiled her sweetest smile and
went straight over to hug him. We see a lot
of Granny because she comes to visit us all
the time, but since Grandpa nearly always
prefers to stay at home we tend to see him
a lot less. I always feel a little bit shy when
I first see Grandpa again, and I think Saffie
probably does too.

'So, Henry,' Dad teased. 'I bet you thought you were going to have a nice peaceful summer, didn't you?'

'Oh, don't worry about him,' Granny joked before Grandpa could reply. 'He never gets any peace in any case living with me, do you, dear?' She beckoned to all of us to follow her into the house. 'Come on. I want to show you my new super-high fencing out the back. You really should get some for your garden, Jim. It's ideal for obscuring the view of the neighbours – though it does rather block out the sun as well.'

'Aren't you worried about your neighbours *hearing* things, Harriet?' Dad asked, and I knew he was thinking about the noise her twelve garden gnomes make whenever they are animated.

'Yes, well, my neighbour on one side

is rather deaf, which helps,' Granny said lightly, 'and the other side think I talk to my plants . . . and to my gnomes, of course . . . I tell Henry to encourage them to think I'm a little bit . . . well . . . you know . . .'

'Bonkers?' Dad supplied helpfully.

'I was going to say *eccentric*,' Granny said, narrowing her eyes at him. 'I also told Henry to spread the word that I'm a retired ventriloquist — just in case they think it's odd that the plants and gnomes talk back. Now, let's all go inside and have a nice cup of tea, shall we?'

'Aren't you coming, Dad?' Mum asked as Grandpa turned to go back inside the garage.

'I've just got to finish off a tricky bit first,' Grandpa said. 'It won't take me long.'

I waited behind as everyone else headed for the house. Dad turned round when he reached the door and called out, 'Come on, Emma. Grandpa doesn't want anyone interfering with his top-secret project.'

Grandpa nodded. 'Sorry, Emmeline, no one's allowed to see what I'm making until it's finished. Don't worry though. All will be revealed in a day or two.'

'But I'm really good at keeping secrets,' I whispered. 'Please can I just have a *little* peek?'

'I'm afraid not, Emmeline. Not even your grandmother has seen it yet!' And Grandpa gave me a little wink as he disappeared inside the garage and shut the door.

I felt a bit annoyed then, and not just because he wouldn't let me see what he was doing. He had called me by my proper name, which everybody else in the family knows I hate. Grandpa really didn't know me – or

Saffie – very well at all, I thought. Still . . . maybe this holiday would change that.

'I must say I was amazed when Dad said he wasn't going to bother with the allotment this year because he was too busy working on this new project,' Mum was saying to Granny as I joined them in the kitchen. 'So when do we actually get to *see* it?'

They were standing by the kettle, and through the window I could see Dad and Saffie out in the back garden. Granny was right, I thought. Their new fencing *was* mega-high and I thought it made their large garden look a lot smaller.

'He says he'll have it finished by Friday, when you and Jim come back for his birthday,' Granny replied. 'Now . . . about the present . . .'

'Cedric!' An excited shriek came from outside as my sister spotted her favourite gnome over by Granny's garden pond. Cedric is a fishing gnome with a very friendly face, bright blue eyes, white hair and a long white beard. He wears green dungarees, black boots and an orange pointy hat and he carries a fishing rod with a grey plastic fish dangling from the end.

Dad took several nervous steps backwards as Saffie brought Cedric to life. Cedric's fish came to life too, flapping away furiously on the end of the line.

'There!' Cedric exclaimed as he threw his fish into the pond where it could swim around freely. He wiped his hands clean on the front of his dungarees as he turned to grin at my sister.

'Cedric, let's have a game of frisbee!' Saffie suggested at once.

Cedric beamed. He was really good at frisbee – something my sister had recently discovered and which had elevated him above Walter to his current position as her favourite gnome.

'Tell you what – I'll go and get the frisbee from the car, shall I?' Dad mumbled, looking relieved to escape.

'What's wrong, Jim? You're not scared of Cedric, are you?' Mum asked mischievously as Dad came into the kitchen.

Dad pulled a face. 'Those gnomes just give me the creeps, that's all. Especially when I'm that close to one.'

'Really, Jim,' Granny said, sounding a bit offended. 'It's not as if you've never seen one of my garden gnomes come to life before!'

Dad gave her a half-amused look. 'Harriet, there are some things a person *never* gets used to, no matter how many times they see it. And I do believe that talking garden gnomes may be one of them!'

CHAPTER 3

For the first two days at Granny and
Grandpa's, Saffie and I were kept really
busy. Granny took us to the park and to
the shops and to visit a friend of hers whose
grandchildren were also staying.

On the third day, however, Granny
hadn't organized anything special for us to
do, and by late morning Saffie was already
complaining of feeling bored. I was pretty
sure Saffie was also starting to miss Mum and
Dad, though of course she wouldn't admit
it. Fortunately there were only two more

days to go until Grandpa's birthday, when our parents were coming back again to stay for the whole weekend.

'What are we going to *do* on Grandpa's birthday if we can't have a party?' Saffie asked me glumly as the daisy chain she was making broke yet again. Saffie is always too rough with delicate things like daisy chains and in the end she nearly always loses patience and gives up.

'I don't know,' I said, taking her broken chain to finish it for her. 'I expect we'll all go out for lunch together or something.'

'Is that *all*?' Saffie was scowling as she plucked impatiently at the grass on the front lawn. She paused before adding, 'I don't see why we can't have just a *little* party.'

'Grown-ups don't usually *have* birthday parties, Saffie,' I told her.

'They do if there's an "O" in their age!' Saffie said stubbornly. 'Daddy told me that's why he had that big party when he was forty.'

'Yes, but Dad *likes* parties. Grandpa doesn't, because he's shy, remember.'

Saffie just scowled even more. She's never really understood what being shy means. She *loves* being the centre of attention herself and is only too happy to have everyone looking at her and listening to her the whole time whenever she's in the room.

'I don't *care* about going out to lunch!' she declared crossly. 'If there isn't a party it won't be a proper birthday!'

Now *I* was starting to get impatient. 'Look, Saffie, it's Grandpa's birthday not yours, so it only matters what *he* wants, not what *you* want! Stop acting like such a baby!'

37

'I am *not* a baby and you're not allowed to say I am!' she shouted, and she stomped off into the house to tell Granny I was calling her names.

'OK, let's give you girls a little time apart, shall we?' Granny said after I'd followed her inside to defend myself. 'Now . . . Saffie . . . why don't you go and look for Cedric in the back garden? I'm sure he'd like another game of frisbee. And Emma –' she waited until my sister had gone outside before continuing – 'come upstairs with me, will you? I've got something I want to show you.'

Granny and Grandpa have a very small room next to their bedroom, which they use for storing things. They call it their box room and it's always kept locked. Granny

38

says it's packed full of delicate stuff and she doesn't want us to accidently break something.

I could hardly believe it that morning when she unlocked the door and actually *invited me in.*

She must have seen the look of surprise on my face because she said quickly, 'You're getting older now and I know you'll be careful not to touch anything . . . but you'd better not mention this to your sister.'

I nodded, even more thrilled that I was being allowed to do something my little sister wasn't.

The curtains had been drawn to keep out the light, and Granny quickly stepped over a pile of dusty books and yanked the curtains back so that we could see better. She must have spotted Saffie in the garden as she looked out of the window, because she let out an exasperated sigh and told me she'd be back in a minute after she'd sorted her out.

After she'd left the room I went to look out of the window myself and couldn't help smiling when I saw what Saffie was doing. She had animated some of the clothes on

Granny's washing line and now they were dancing about in the garden. Granny's big pants looked especially funny as they tried to join in the game of frisbee.

I turned my attention back to the room I was in. There were several shelves on the walls, most of them filled with small or half-finished model cars and aeroplanes. (Grandpa's best work was on show in a proper display cabinet downstairs.)

There were a lot of cardboard boxes on the floor, some taped shut and some with things poking out the top of them. My gaze fell on what looked like a large doll, half wrapped in tissue paper, sticking out from one of the boxes. I went over and carefully eased her out of the box.

'Wow!' I said out loud after removing the paper, because the doll was really beautiful.

She looked quite old, and at first I wondered if, like Elvira, she had once belonged to Mum. Then I thought that, if she had, Mum would definitely have told us about her. This doll was a lot bigger than Elvira and she had a very beautiful shiny

face. She had amazing sapphire-blue opening-and-closing eyes, long dark eyelashes, rosy cheeks and a pink, bow-shaped mouth. Her goldy-brown hair was shoulder-length and styled in ringlets. She was dressed in a long lacy cream gown with a red velvet sash tied around the middle. On her feet she wore white ankle socks and sweet little red leather shoes with red straps.

I must have stood there for ages with the doll in my arms, lost in a bit of a daydream as I let my imagination carry me away. The doll looked beautiful enough to have once belonged to a princess, I thought. Perhaps the princess and the doll had worn identical clothes and the princess had taken the doll everywhere with her until one day the doll had been lost and . . .

'*Emma!*' Granny's cross voice made me jump. 'Put that back at once!'

I was shocked. Granny usually only sounds like that if she thinks we're about to do something dangerous like touch a hot oven or run out into the road without looking.

43

I put the doll back into her box so hastily that the box tipped up and the doll nearly toppled out again on to the floor. I felt tears sting my eyes. Why was Granny so angry?

Granny took one look at my face and quickly told me she was sorry for shouting. 'I didn't mean to scare you, Emma. I'd forgotten that doll was in here and it gave me quite a fright to see you holding her.'

'Why? Is she very fragile or something?' The doll looked pretty robust to me – much more robust than Elvira – but maybe I was missing something.

'Not really . . .'

'So why can't I touch her?' I asked.

'I was afraid you might bring her to life,' Granny said, 'and this is a doll who must never be brought to life again.'

'Why not?' I was even more curious now.

'Hasn't your mother ever mentioned Queenie-May?' Granny asked.

I shook my head in surprise. 'Was she Mum's doll then?'

'Oh, no . . . Queenie-May is much older than that. She belonged to my sister Penelope when we were children.'

'Penelope? You don't mean *Great-Aunt* Penelope who was killed by a dinosaur?' I blurted out excitedly.

'Yes, I do mean her, and I wish you wouldn't sound quite so thrilled when you talk about her tragic and untimely death, Emma,' Granny said sternly.

'Sorry, Granny,' I said at once. But that still didn't stop me feeling even more intrigued. I knew that Penelope had been Granny's eccentric older sister who had believed in 'throwing caution to the wind'

45

when it came to using her superpower. And I knew she had been killed years before I was born in what Mum always described as 'a tragic accident in a dinosaur museum'. Mum never liked talking about her aunt's death, except to impress on us that it could easily have been avoided if Great-Aunt Penelope hadn't decided to bring to life a gigantic model of a pterodactyl and fly around the room on its back.

'Penelope and I used to bring Queenie-May to life an awful lot when we were little,' Granny explained now, 'and since we were both extremely strong-willed little girls I'm afraid that in time Queenie-May became a doll with a very strong personality of her own. Eventually she became far *too* powerful when she was animated – too out-of-control for her animator to handle in fact.'

I looked at Granny in surprise. I knew that toys tended to have their own personalities as well as being influenced by the personality of the person (or people) who brought them to life. And I also knew that the more often a toy was animated the stronger its personality became. But this was the first I'd heard of a brought-to-life toy being so powerful that its animator couldn't stay in control of it.

'Now . . . I want you to forget you ever saw this doll and you must promise not to mention any of it to your sister,' Granny said briskly.

'But—' I still had lots of questions, but Granny interrupted me.

'Now, Emma, come over here, will you? *This* is the toy I wanted you to see!' And with a dramatic flourish she yanked the dust cover from the top of a large doll's house.

'Wow!' I exclaimed in delight. I had always loved doll's houses and this was a very beautiful one.

'Grandpa made this for your mum when she was your age,' Granny told me, smiling.

The wooden house was double-fronted, with two storeys and a high-peaked red shiny roof. There were five windows, all with yellow metal shutters, and the yellow front door was framed by a sweet little porch. The front of the house had rambling roses painted all over it.

'I love it!' I declared, and Granny immediately suggested we took it downstairs so that I could look at it properly.

But we were both so concerned with getting the doll's house out of the room without dropping it that neither of us noticed Granny had forgotten to lock the door behind us.

CHAPTER 4

Granny set the doll's house down on the
kitchen table and showed me how the front
swung open in two sections.

The house had been partitioned off into
six rooms, with a staircase connecting the
two levels. The loose furniture and the dolls
were all jumbled up inside, but it was still
easy to see how gorgeous it was.

Each room was decorated with a different
wallpaper. There was flowery pink in the
main bedroom, stripy gold-and-red for the
living room downstairs and a paper that

50

looked like tiny tiles for the bathroom. The floors were all carpeted, apart from the kitchen, which had yellow lino. Miniature curtains were hanging at the windows and there were little mini-paintings on some of the walls. All the rooms had lights hanging from the ceiling, and on the landing there was even a tiny glass chandelier. An oval mirror with a gold frame had been fixed on to the nearby wall so that the chandelier was reflected in it.

'Wow!' I exclaimed in delight. 'It's beautiful.'

'Your grandpa always was one for attention to detail,' Granny said with a smile. 'Do you think you can sort out all the furniture?'

'Of course!' I said.

'Good. You see I want you to use this doll's house to practise *your* animation

skills, Emma. Believe me it requires a lot of concentration and practice to become good at such dainty animation. I've never been very good at it myself and I don't think it's really Saffie's thing either.'

I was a bit surprised. 'But if it's too

difficult for you and Saffie then it's going to
be *far* too hard for me,' I said.

'Nonsense! You should learn to have more
confidence in yourself, Emma! Now . . . I
think I'd better go and check on your sister.'

After she'd gone outside I slowly started

to sort out the doll's house. All the furniture had been knocked over, so I began by taking everything out so that I could put back all the pieces where I thought they should go. I began by finding all the items that belonged in the bathroom. There was a blue bath with tiny gold-painted taps, a matching blue sink and a teeny toilet with a gold seat. I also found a wooden towel rack with a miniature towel glued on to it and a matching bath-mat.

The kitchen was next. I had already spotted a cute plastic fridge that opened to reveal two movable shelves, a miniature milk bottle and a wedge of cheese inside. There was a little cooker, a table and chairs, and several loose pots and pans.

Granny came back into the kitchen with Saffie while I was inspecting a sweet little dressing table which had a real mirror and drawers that you could actually open.

'Emma, what are you doing?!' Granny exclaimed. 'The object of this exercise is for you to get the *dolls* to tidy up the house.'

Saffie let out a gasp of delight as she rushed to join me. 'You have to do it like *this*, Emma!' And she promptly focused on a small plastic doll wearing a plain dress and a floral apron, lying under an upturned table.

'Careful, Saffie,' Granny warned as the doll leaped up so high she banged her head on the kitchen ceiling and let out a scream as the table flew across the room to crash into the wall. 'Don't blast her with your power. Concentrate on delivering it slowly and steadily – that's what tiny objects need so they can function properly.'

Saffie looked like she was struggling to

keep her power reined in as the mother doll made her way clumsily across the rest of the ground floor of the doll's house, wading through furniture and bashing into everything as she went. As she approached a baby doll lying on the floor in the living room, Granny said, 'OK, Saffie, let Emma take over now before something gets broken. Come on, Emma. Show us how it's done!'

'But . . . but I won't be able to do it better than Saffie . . .' I said nervously.

'Just try,' Granny said firmly.

So I tentatively fixed my gaze on the mum doll, which had fallen back on to the floor as soon as Saffie had stopped animating it.

This is the part that's hard to explain. Basically to bring something to life you have to sort of mentally *zap* it into action. It's hard to describe to someone who hasn't got a superpower, but basically what I feel is a sort of funny 'ping' inside my head just before the animation happens, like a spring being released or an elastic band being snapped or something like that.

I felt the 'ping' now just before the mum doll stood up again. I watched as she rubbed her head, then spotted her baby and rushed over to lift it up. She began rocking it in her arms. As soon as the mother picked up her baby I found that I was able to animate that too without any extra effort. I forgot everything else as I kept focusing on the little doll's-house

figures, watching as the mother gently placed the baby inside its crib and covered it with a tiny white square of knitted blanket before beginning to tidy up the rest of the house.

'Wow!' Saffie exclaimed. 'You did that much better than me!'

I looked across at Granny, who was smiling at me proudly.

'I don't know how . . .' I began, trailing off.

Granny smiled. 'I told you, Emma. It's not true that your power is weaker than Saffie's. Your power is *different*, that's all!'

I felt a sort of warm fuzzy feeling in my middle as she said that. It had never occurred to me before that there might be any sort of animation I could do more easily than my sister.

★

That night I was fast asleep, in the middle of
a lovely dream where I was playing with a
doll's house full of teddy bears, when I felt
my arm being shaken.

'Saffie?' I murmured
groggily, before turning
on the bedside light and
letting out a little shriek
of surprise. Howard was
standing beside my bed
wearing a pink cone-
shaped party hat with
streamers decorating
the top.

'I'm sorry, Emma,'
he said in his soft
growly voice. 'I
wanted to wake

you as soon as Saffie brought me to life, but there wasn't time.'

'Saffie?' I hissed, automatically turning to look at my sister's bed. It was empty and her duvet was half on the bed and half off it.

'Elvira and Dorothy and two of the gnomes are out in the garden with us and we're having a midnight feast,' Howard continued. 'Saffie sent me to fetch some biscuits from the kitchen, but I thought it would be better if I fetched you instead.' He frowned. 'Does this hat look *very* ridiculous? Saffie says I have to keep it on or I'll be a party pooper. I don't know what that is, but it doesn't sound very pleasant.' He seemed worried as he added, 'I do so dislike looking ridiculous, because as you know I am a very *sensible* sort of bear.'

'I think you look cute,' I told him. 'But you don't have to wear it if you don't want to.'

I suddenly realized something. 'Hey, how is Saffie animating you when she can't *see* you?'

'I believe your grandmother calls the technique "blind" animating. Anyway, whatever it's called I'm afraid she's been teaching Saffie how to do it.' As he carefully eased the hat elastic out from under his chin he added with a yawn, 'I think I'd like to go back to sleep now.'

'That's fine. You do that.' I quickly went over to the window and looked down into the back garden.

'They're in the *front* garden,' Howard said at once.

'The *front* garden?' I was shocked.

61

I got downstairs to find the front door wide open and the porch light on. It was like a beacon signalling to any neighbours who happened to be awake to look this way, I thought crossly.

Saffie, Elvira, Dorothy and Cedric were all sitting cross-legged in a circle on Granny's picnic rug with various

bits of food set out in front of them on Granny's best china plates.

Walter was standing on his upturned wheelbarrow over by the hedge, inspecting one of the hedge statues. Walter has white hair, a long white beard and a pair of round metal-rimmed glasses perched on the end of his nose. In his plastic form he's holding his wheelbarrow, but whenever he comes to life he gets one of the other gnomes to push it for him because he says it aggravates his bad back. 'Really, Miss Serafina, I must say I'm surprised at you!' he was saying sternly as he pushed his glasses further back on to his nose. 'It's lucky this peacock is still in one piece. You cannot bring a hedge sculpture to life when it is still attached to the rest of the hedge. You could have uprooted the whole thing!'

Saffie's face was hilarious. She clearly didn't appreciate being told off by Walter, who she had always thought of as an admirer until now.

'I think you *should* uproot the hedge, Saffie!' Dorothy (Saffie's red-haired rag doll) suddenly declared, standing up and adjusting her party hat. 'Think how funny a flying hedge would look! You could easily do it. You brought a garden shed to life before without any trouble, didn't you?' She stopped abruptly as she saw me standing on the porch. 'Uh-oh . . .'

I ignored her and glared at my sister as she turned and saw me too. 'Saffie, what are you *doing* out here? Anyone could be watching and you know you're not allowed to be out the front on your own! And *why* are you using Granny's best tea-plates?'

Saffie gave me an angelic smile. 'Don't be cross, Emma. We were going to have our midnight feast in the back garden, but Elvira and Dorothy wanted to see the hedge sculptures, so we came out here instead. I tried to bring the peacock to life, but it went a bit wrong. Elvira chose the plates. She said we had to have them to make the cucumber sandwiches look pretty.' She paused for a moment. 'Have you seen Howard? He was meant to be bringing biscuits.'

'He came to find me instead,' I grunted.

'*What?*' Saffie looked irritated. 'Howard *never* does what I tell him to. He's *such* a naughty bear!'

I couldn't help laughing. 'He never does what you tell him to because he's such a *good* bear!' I corrected her. 'Come on, let's go inside before someone sees us.'

'Coming out front was Elvira's idea, not mine,' Dorothy announced suddenly. 'Elvira is *always* getting poor Saffie into trouble.' She gave Elvira a superior look. 'I'm sure Saffie would get rid of you if you weren't some old relic who used to belong to her mother.'

'That's not true!' the china doll retorted hotly. 'And the only reason she doesn't give *you* away, Dorothy, is that nobody would want you with that *dish-mop* hair. In fact, if we turned you upside down and dipped you in some water we could use you to mop the floor! Tee-hee!'

'Will you two stop it!' I snapped, seeing that nothing had changed between Saffie's two dolls just because they were away from home.

But instead of listening they started to

hurl things at each other, throwing anything they could get their hands on – including Granny's best china plates.

CHAPTER 5

Elvira ducked just in time as the first plate whizzed right over her head to land with a crash on the front path.

'Stop it!' I yelled. I quickly switched off the porch light and hustled Saffie and the dolls inside as Granny's voice shouted down to us from the top of the stairs.

'GIRLS, IS THAT YOU? WHAT *IS* GOING ON DOWN THERE?'

Granny was furious when she found out about her broken plate, and even more so when she heard how it had happened. Saffie had quickly de-animated the gnomes and the dolls when we'd heard Granny coming, and Elvira and Dorothy were now lying innocently on the sofa. But that didn't stop Granny glaring daggers at them.

'Your mother told me she would only let you bring *one* of those dolls,' Granny challenged my sister sharply. 'So why are they *both* here?'

In a small voice Saffie told Granny how she had sneaked Dorothy into the car at the last minute. 'I was afraid she'd be lonely left at home all on her own,' she finished. 'Wasn't I, Emma?'

I nodded, wishing now that I'd told Mum about the extra doll in the first place.

'I see . . . well . . .' Granny gave us both a stern look. 'Dorothy and Elvira can *both* go home with your parents on Sunday. Until then I shall put them away somewhere safe.' As she saw Saffie's expression she added, 'Don't worry, Saffie. I'm sure your mother will let you have them back at the end of the holiday if you behave yourself while you're here.'

I knew Granny was doing this for Saffie's own good — as well as for the good of her best china crockery — but Saffie clearly didn't see it that way. When we went back upstairs Saffie climbed into her bed with a face like thunder.

'Saffie,' I whispered after Granny had turned out our bedroom light and closed the door. 'Are you OK?'

She didn't reply apart from a sniff, and I was afraid she might be crying.

'We can still bring Howard to life,' I whispered. My teddy bear was no longer

animated, which wasn't surprising since
Saffie had clearly forgotten all about him.
'Howard won't get us into any trouble with
Granny. He's too—'

'Boring?' Saffie hissed without looking
up.

'*Sensible*,' I corrected her crossly, and I
went to sleep deciding that I needn't feel too
worried about her after all.

The following morning at breakfast time
Granny seemed back to her normal cheerful
self until Saffie said, 'I promise I'll be really
good from now on, Granny, so can I *please*
have my dolls back?'

'I don't think that would be very wise,
Saffie,' Granny replied.

'Well, just one of them then?' Saffie
pleaded. '*Please?*'

'No, Saffie. Eat your breakfast or that boiled egg will go cold.'

Saffie put down her spoon. 'Granny, *where* have you put my dolls?' she demanded.

'Serafina,' Grandpa broke in, actually lowering his newspaper at the breakfast table, which he practically never does. 'Granny told me what happened last night and I think she's absolutely right. Now be a good girl and stop hounding her and eat up your breakfast.'

Of course, after that Saffie made a big thing of *not* eating her breakfast. She sat at the table in complete silence with her darkest scowl on her face and as soon as Grandpa went out to the garage she got up to leave the table too.

'Just a minute, young lady,' Granny said. The first morning at Granny's I'd offered to help with the washing-up. 'Goodness, no!' she'd exclaimed. 'In *this* house the dishes do themselves!' And this morning was no exception. As she spoke she turned and gave the sink a hard sort of stare. Seconds later the plates and mugs and everything else in the washing-up bowl had grown little arms and were vigorously scrubbing themselves.

Even Saffie started to giggle, and not for the first time I wished that Mum would let us bring the dishes to life at home.

Granny told Saffie she wanted to take her to the park that morning to practise using her superpower *discreetly* outside. Saffie clearly liked the idea too much to say no, even if she was still in a bad mood.

'Saffie, I think you should change into some normal clothes before we go out,'

Granny added, frowning at my sister's Supergirl outfit and in particular at the tomato-ketchup stain on her yellow leotard.

Saffie narrowed her eyes as she stated emphatically, 'But I want to wear this.'

Granny sighed. 'Very well then. Emma, we should be back by lunchtime, and Grandpa is in the garage if you need him.'

I nodded, because I was more than happy to be left on my own to play some more with Mum's old doll's house.

For the next hour or so I was totally caught up in my own little world. After setting the dolls to one side I finished sorting out the furniture inside the house – by hand rather than by animation. When I had all the rooms just how I wanted them I decided it was time to let the dolls move back in.

In addition to the mum and baby doll, there was a daddy doll dressed in a brown felt suit, two identical little girl dolls with brown curly hair and faded pink dresses, and a boy doll dressed in little blue shorts and a red top. There was also a stern-looking adult female doll in a black dress with a grey bun who I decided must be the nanny.

The thing about animating toys is that once you've brought them to life they sort of act independently. It's not that you can't

influence the way they behave at all – if you're a calm person in a calm mood then the doll you animate will probably be calm too. And of course the opposite applies if you're angry. But aside from that an object that already has some kind of character – a doll with a cheeky face for instance – will tend to behave in keeping with that. In the case of my doll's-house family I knew that the nanny would be strict and the children would all be mischievous. And I knew that as soon as I put the family back inside the house and brought them to life I would be setting off a little adventure that I could sit back and watch, as well as actually take part in if I wanted to. (Of course, I would seem like a giant to the doll's-house family – but at least I'd be a friendly giant.)

I decided it would be fun to place the

family in their beds before I 'woke' them up. The bedroom for the mum and dad dolls had a wooden double bed with a cover made from a square of white handkerchief material. The baby's little pink plastic crib was in there as well.

The other upstairs bedroom was the nursery. It had red wooden bunk beds with orange covers, and two other single beds, a small red wooden one for the little boy, and a longer bed with a pretty floral cover for the nanny. Next to the nanny's bed was a rocking chair with a tiny orange cushion to sit on. There was also a little white bookcase with some miniature books on the shelves, a cute plastic rocking horse, a teeny toy car and a tiny teddy bear. I had also squeezed in the fish tank since I couldn't find any space for it elsewhere, and a plastic cat with two kittens in a basket.

After all the dolls were lying down in their beds I sat back and concentrated on animating them. I wasn't sure how many I could bring to life at the same time, so I was really pleased when I managed to do them all. I guessed that when it came to animating very small things, a little superpower went a long way.

It gave me an excited tingly feeling inside as I watched all the dolls waking up. I'd even managed to animate the cats and the fish. Of course, I could have animated the furniture itself, but I didn't want to do that, at least not at the moment. For now I just wanted to concentrate on getting to know the family. I had thought about giving them names, but then I'd realized that Mum must already have done that and I thought it might be nice to use the same ones.

The baby woke up first and started crying loudly. The mum and dad dolls woke up then and the mum picked up the baby and gave it a cuddle.

At the same time in the other bedroom the nanny woke and started to shout at the children to get up or they'd be late.

'Late for what?' the children all shouted together, but the nanny didn't seem to know.

The nanny was tutting loudly to herself as she spotted the fish tank. 'I must get your father to take this downstairs. Never in all my years as a nanny have I had a fish tank in the bedroom. I'm sure one could catch all manner of diseases from it.'

'What sorts of diseases?' the children asked, but again the nanny didn't seem to have an answer.

The little boy went to have a ride on the rocking horse and the twin girls were soon on their way into the other bedroom to see the baby. Meanwhile the kittens started chasing each other round the floor, nearly tripping up the nanny.

Since none of them seemed to have noticed me I decided it would be better to keep it that way for a while. I wasn't sure that I was quite ready yet to play the part of the friendly giant.

★

Grandpa found me sitting with the doll's house at the kitchen table when he came in from the garage to make himself a cup of tea.

'It's nice to see that old doll's house getting some attention again, Emmeline,' he said. 'I remember your mother used to spend hours at a time with it when she was your age.'

'Did Granny make the dolls come alive for her?' I asked curiously.

Grandpa shook his head. 'Your mother wouldn't let her interfere.' He chuckled at the memory. 'Marsha always insisted on playing with it in a normal way, making up little voices for the dolls . . . all that sort of thing.'

'I wonder why,' I said in surprise. I couldn't think of anything more exciting than having a doll's house with real live little people inside it.

'Oh, I expect she wanted to bring it to life using her imagination,' Grandpa said. 'That way it could be her own little world that *she* was in charge of rather than your grandmother . . .' There was something in his voice that made me think his opinion came from personal experience.

I suddenly decided to ask him something that had been bugging me for a while. 'Grandpa, why do you keep calling me Emmeline? Nobody else does . . . except Mum when she's cross with me. And I really don't like being called it.' I felt my face flushing a little, but I kept looking at him.

'I'm sorry!' Grandpa looked taken aback. '*I've* always thought it a beautiful name. Call me a fanciful old man if you like, but it makes me think of someone special, like a queen. *Queen Emmeline* . . . But I'll try to remember to call you Emma if you'd like that better.'

'Yes please,' I said. 'I would.' But I smiled, because I felt quite flattered by his answer.

'Now . . .' Grandpa said, looking at his watch. 'Where can your sister and grandmother have got to? I do hope nothing's gone wrong.'

CHAPTER 6

'I'll never be able to show my face in that supermarket ever again!' Granny complained as she walked in through the front door half an hour later.

'I've brought things to life in the supermarket with Mummy before, and she *always* shows her face there again,' Saffie protested crossly as she followed behind Granny. 'Anyway, you shouldn't have kicked Trevor.'

'Trevor?'

'Our trolley, of course! He had a sweet

little face as well, only you didn't even see it!'

My sister pulled her Supergirl cape straighter on her shoulders before stomping off upstairs.

It turned out that after the park Granny had taken Saffie to the supermarket, where Saffie had decided to bring their shopping trolley to life.

'It had one of those irritating front wheels that keep getting stuck,' Granny explained. 'I gave it a kick to unjam it and it yelled, "HOW DARE YOU KICK MY WONKY WHEEL, YOU HORRIBLE OLD LADY!" I got such a fright I think I actually screamed.'

'Oh dear,' Grandpa said, trying not to laugh as he told Granny that now she knew how *he* felt when she brought something of *his* to life unexpectedly.

Granny ignored him and turned her attention to me. 'Well, Emma, this afternoon it will be *your* turn to learn something new.'

'Can you teach me "blind" animating?' I asked before she had time to suggest anything else.

'Of course!' Granny looked pleased that I was so interested. 'We'll begin straight away after lunch.' And she immediately brought the kitchen table to life and asked it to get on with laying itself while she prepared us something to eat.

That afternoon, while Saffie continued to sulk in our room, Granny took me into the back garden and told me to have a good look at Cedric.

'With blind animating the most important

part is *picturing* the object in your head,'
Granny told me. 'It can be quite difficult
unless the object is one you know extremely
well.'

Afterwards, when I was ready, I had to go
inside and sit on the sofa with my eyes shut,
doing my best to see Cedric's face in my
mind's eye as I focused my superpower on
bringing him to life.

I was amazed when I felt the familiar
'ping' inside my head that meant I was using
my superpower. Soon Granny was telling
me that Cedric had just thrown his fish into
the garden pond and was now settling down
happily to engage in his favourite pastime of
trying to fish it out again.

I went outside to have a look for
myself and at the same time I glanced up
at our bedroom window to see if Saffie

was looking out. Briefly I thought I saw movement at the other window – the box-room one – but then I thought I must have imagined it.

Grandpa was entering the back garden through the side gate, a strange smile on his face.

'I have an announcement to make, ladies,' he said in an important-sounding voice.

'It's never finished?' Granny asked at once, looking as if that was the last thing she'd expected.

'It is!' Grandpa declared triumphantly.

'You mean we're actually allowed into the garage to see your secret project, Grandpa?'

'That's right, Emmeline . . . I mean, Emma.'

'I'd better tell Saffie!' I said excitedly.

As Grandpa led Granny towards the garage I went back inside the house and yelled upstairs to my sister. 'Saffie! We're allowed to see what Grandpa's been making! Are you coming?'

'I'm busy,' came the muffled reply.

I sighed and decided to leave her to it.

I hurried back outside and caught up with my grandparents at the side door of the garage, where Granny was standing absolutely still as she looked inside.

'Oh, *Henry*!' she exclaimed eventually, letting out a funny noise somewhere between a gasp of surprise and a delighted laugh. She didn't seem able to say anything else.

'WOW!' I exclaimed after I had squeezed past her to have a look myself. Taking up one half of the garage was a *massive* model

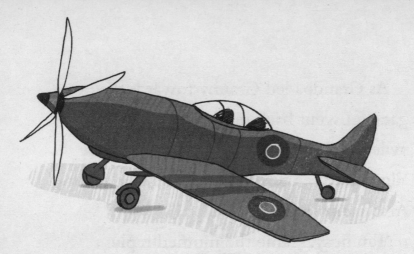

aeroplane. Grandpa had never made a model anywhere near as big or as detailed as this before. It wasn't anything like the ones displayed in his cabinet. It didn't really look like a model at all, but more like a mini version of a real plane – the old-fashioned kind you see in museums or being flown in air displays sometimes. It was a greeny-grey colour with red and blue targets painted on the wings and sides, and a big propeller on the front. There was a cockpit with seats for the pilot and one passenger sitting directly behind and it even had a proper sliding roof.

'It's a replica of a famous plane called the "Spitfire" which was flown in the Second World War,' Grandpa explained proudly. 'It's exactly a sixth of the real size.'

'It's amazing!' I blurted, briefly remembering Mum telling me that our great-grandfather had been killed in the Second World War when Grandpa was just a baby. 'Grandpa, did you *really* make this all by yourself?'

'I certainly did,' he replied with a chuckle. 'No gnomes are allowed in this garage, I can assure you!'

'My gnomes couldn't do this even if they *were* allowed in,' Granny murmured.

Grandpa promptly grinned from ear to ear, clearly delighted by her comment. 'Not even Walter?'

'Not even Walter,' she said firmly. 'I have

91

to admit that I'm amazed, Henry. Really amazed.' And she was looking at Grandpa in an entirely new way – as if she had just discovered that *he* had a special power too.

When I eventually decided to go upstairs and check on Saffie I found her trying to hide something under her bed.

'Saffie, what are you doing?' I asked suspiciously.

'Oh . . . nothing really . . .'

'Saffie . . .' I began sternly.

'Oh, all right, but you have to promise not to tell.' And she slid out Queenie-May.

'Saffie!' I almost shrieked. 'What are you doing with that doll?'

She looked surprised by my reaction. 'I was looking for Elvira and Dorothy. The little spare room wasn't locked, so I went inside. I found her in one of the boxes. Isn't she beautiful?' Saffie was stroking the doll's hair lovingly.

'Oh, Saffie . . . you'll have to put her back,' I said. 'Granny says we're not allowed to play with her.' And I told her everything Granny had told me about Queenie-May.

'But that's just silly,' Saffie challenged at once. 'Even if she *is* a very strong-willed doll we can always just de-animate her if she starts doing something *really* bad.'

'I know, but . . .' I broke off because Saffie was right. We *could* just de-animate her.

My sister was hugging the doll possessively now. 'It's not fair, Emma. All I want to do is play with her. I think it's really cruel of Granny to shut her away like that, even if she *has* been naughty.' Saffie sniffed and I knew she was imagining herself in the doll's place.

'I've got an idea,' I said. 'You can keep Queenie-May here if you promise you won't bring her to life until I've asked Granny a bit more about her.'

Saffie beamed. 'Emma, you're the best big sister in the whole world!' And she came over and gave me a big hug.

I grinned. She really can be very sweet when she gets what she wants.

Grandpa was wheeling his plane outside and up on to the front lawn, where it looked even more impressive with the sun shining down on its gleaming paintwork.

'WOW! Can it fly?' Saffie wanted to know as soon as she saw it.

'With an engine it can, yes,' Grandpa

94

replied. 'But that's something that costs an awful lot of money, so I'll have to discuss it with your Granny first.'

'Oh.' Saffie didn't bother to hide her disappointment.

Grandpa didn't seem to mind though. He just chuckled. 'Don't worry. At least the hard part's done.' As a car drew up outside the house he said, 'Oh look . . . here's Donald. He has a plane that *does* have an engine. Maybe he'll let you see it fly if you ask him nicely, Saffie.' (Donald was Grandpa's friend and fellow model-maker and he'd been the only person allowed in the garage the whole time Grandpa was building his plane.)

As we hadn't seen Donald in over a year it took a while for him to stop going on about how much Saffie and I had grown.

95

Then Saffie asked if it was OK to ask him a question that *wasn't* about models.

Donald gave a little laugh and said of course.

'Donald, did you have a birthday party when you were seventy?' my sister asked in her most serious grown-up voice.

Donald told her with a smile that he was only sixty-three.

'Oh . . .' But Saffie wasn't deterred for long. 'I bet you *like* birthday parties though, don't you? Not like Grandpa!'

Donald looked at our grandfather in amusement. 'Don't you like a party then, Henry?' he teased.

'I hated them even when I was a lad,' Grandpa replied with feeling, looking more at Saffie and me than at Donald. 'I was really shy, you see, and I found it a bit scary mixing with lots of other children who all seemed much more confident than me. And then there was the jelly problem.'

'The *jelly* problem?' Saffie and I queried in unison.

'Yes. You see you nearly always got given jelly at children's parties in those days and my older brother had once told me that jelly was made from boiled slugs.'

'Yuck!' Saffie and I burst out.

'Of course, I didn't really believe him once I got older, but by then I couldn't put a spoonful of jelly in my mouth without it turning my stomach.'

'Grandpa, that's horrible!' I exclaimed, while Saffie just looked at him wide-eyed.

He nodded in agreement. 'What made it worse was that I was too shy to actually *say* I didn't like jelly, so I always got it dished out to me at birthday parties. And since my mother had taught me that it was rude not to clear my plate, I always got very stressed about what to do with it.'

'What *did* you do with it?' Saffie asked curiously.

'If I was lucky another child might eat it for me. Or if not I'd secretly spoon it into my trouser pockets.'

'Yuck!' Saffie and I said again as Donald let out an amused snort.

'That's nothing compared to the time I actually forced myself to eat some,' Grandpa continued. 'I tried not to think about slugs as I was swallowing it, but I quickly started to feel queasy. I was too shy to tell anyone of course, and I ended up being sick all over the table in the middle of everybody singing "Happy Birthday".'

98

'Grandpa, that's disgusting!' I declared, pulling a face.

'I'm surprised anyone invited you to a party again after that,' Donald said with a frown.

My sister was looking at Grandpa in astonishment. She clearly couldn't imagine any little boy being too shy to say that he didn't like jelly – or that he felt sick and needed to leave the table.

'Poor Grandpa,' she suddenly burst out passionately, rushing over to give him a sympathetic hug. As he hugged her back she confided, '*I* was sick all over the bed once when we were having a midnight feast at home, wasn't I, Emma? It was *horrible*!'

'It was,' I agreed. 'Especially as it was *my* bed. That's why I've told Saffie I'm not having any more midnight feasts with her.'

'Oh dear,' Grandpa said with a twinkle in his eye. 'I must say I always *loved* midnight feasts when I was a youngster.'

'Really?' Saffie immediately looked super-interested. She seemed to be thinking very hard before finally letting out a contented sigh, then smiling at Grandpa as if she had just had a very pleasing idea.

CHAPTER 7

After Donald had gone home, Grandpa
stayed outside to polish up his plane a bit
more and Saffie stayed with him to help.
I decided now was a good time to try and
speak to Granny. 'Granny, can I ask you
a bit more about Queenie-May?' I asked,
trying to sound as casual as I could.

'Of course, Emma. What do you want to
know?'

'Well . . . did she do any *really* bad things
when you were little?'

'Oh, quite dreadful things sometimes,'

Granny replied without hesitation. 'I've never forgotten what she did to my lovely panda bear just because she was jealous of him. It's true I preferred him to her and probably showed it, but it shouldn't have mattered because she was Penelope's doll in any case. That was the trouble with Queenie-May – she wanted to be *everybody's* favourite.'

'So what did she do?' I prompted, starting to get a bit of a sinking feeling in my stomach.

'Well, we were at the seaside and Penelope had brought Queenie-May with us – she took her everywhere back then. We were on the pier waiting for our mother to come out of the Ladies. It was a cold day and the pier was almost deserted apart from us, so Penelope thought it would be safe to bring Queenie-May to life. That awful doll grabbed my darling Paddy and ran off along the pier with him, shouting that she was going to throw him over the rail.'

'That's terrible,' I exclaimed, thinking how I'd feel if something like that happened to Howard. 'But why didn't you just de-animate her?'

'Because we couldn't! Once we'd brought her to life we couldn't control her any more. She was so powerful we could only de-animate her when *she* let us.'

I gaped at Granny, totally stunned, wondering for a moment if I had heard her correctly.

Granny meanwhile was continuing with the story. 'My poor panda bear would have been lost forever if it hadn't been for my quick-thinking mother. She came back

103

outside just as Queenie-May threw Paddy into the water. There were two men fishing off the pier a little further along – fortunately they had their backs turned to us and hadn't seen Queenie-May. Mother asked if they would help us and one of them had a net and managed to fish Paddy out.'

'Phew,' I said, relieved that at least there was a happy ending. 'But what happened to Queenie-May?'

'Mother got hold of her and threatened to throw *her* in the sea if she didn't let us de-animate her at once. Queenie-May was scared of our mother so she agreed. Mother confiscated her after that and we always thought she was gone for good. We could hardly believe it when we found her at the bottom of an old trunk in our mother's loft when we were sorting through her things after she died. We were both grown-ups by then of course, but Penelope was still delighted to see her old doll again. And years later when Penelope died I couldn't quite bring myself to part with Queenie-May either. She felt like a last connection with my sister I suppose.' She paused. 'But I'd certainly never risk bringing her to life again. And I don't want you girls being tempted to either, which is why I've kept her locked away for all this time.' She paused again. '*Now* do you understand?'

I nodded. I did understand and I felt extremely worried as I hurried out to the front garden to find my sister.

Grandpa was standing on the front lawn talking to the neighbour from across the road, who had come to have a closer look at

the plane. It was the first time I'd ever seen
Grandpa chatting away like that with one of
their neighbours.

'Saffie went back inside,' Grandpa told
me. 'She was getting bored, so I told her to
go and find something else to do.'

I went back into the house and ran up the
stairs as fast as I could. Saffie being bored is
never a good thing.

I pushed open our bedroom door to find
my sister sitting
cross-legged on
her bed.

Queenie-May was sitting next to her with her legs stretched out in front of her. 'Ooh – you *are* a dear,' the doll was saying as she wiggled her toes. 'You've no idea how gorgeous it feels to stretch out one's limbs after all this time.'

I just glared at Saffie.

'Hi, Emma!' Saffie greeted me, looking a bit sheepish. 'I know you said to wait before I brought Queenie-May to life, but you were taking *ages*.'

Queenie-May turned her perfectly painted face in my direction and gave me a smile. 'You may play with me too if you like, Emma. I always encourage sisters to share. The last little girls I lived with – Penelope and Harriet – used to play with me together all the time.'

Saffie giggled. 'Harriet is our granny. And Penelope would have been our great-aunt if she hadn't got killed by a dinosaur in a museum!'

'Killed by a dinosaur! How splendid!' Queenie-May exclaimed in delight. 'Penny always was the adventurous one – that's why she and I got along so well! Now –' she looked from me to Saffie – 'which of *you* is the more adventurous, do you think?'

'I am,' Saffie answered straight away. 'Emma's the sensible one and *I'm* the adventurous one! Everybody says so, don't they, Emma?'

Before I could reply, Queenie-May said with a laugh, 'Excellent! Well, you and I are going to have lots of fun together, Saffie!'

I suddenly found myself feeling extremely protective of my little sister. 'Saffie, I need to talk to you in private,' I said. 'Come out on to the landing for a minute, will you?'

'I'm not sure if I can keep you animated once I leave the room,' Saffie said apologetically to Queenie-May. 'I did with Emma's teddy bear, but I've known him a really long time.'

'Oh, don't worry about that,' Queenie-May replied smoothly. 'I can stay animated all on my own.'

'Really?' Saffie looked shocked.

'Come *on,* Saffie,' I hissed, pulling her towards the door. 'We need to talk *now*.'

I told Saffie in a whisper everything Granny had told me about what had happened all those years ago on the pier – and also what she had said about not being able to de-animate Queenie-May.

Saffie was wide-eyed when I'd finished the story.

'I still think you should go back in there and *try* to de-animate her,' I said.

Saffie nodded and we opened the bedroom door and went back inside, but Queenie-May seemed to have vanished.

'Look,' Saffie said rushing over to the window, which was wide open.

'Saffie, be careful!' I hissed, grabbing hold of her Supergirl cape as she leaned out. The cape came off in my hand and I quickly grabbed on to the back of her leotard instead.

'I bet she climbed down that ivy,' Saffie said, pointing at the tangle of green tendrils growing up the wall.

I pulled my sister back inside the room so that I could have a look myself. The ivy she had spotted was close to the window, but it didn't look strong enough to take even a

110

child's weight.
However,
Queenie-
May was
much lighter
than a child.

'Emma,
where's
Howard?'
Saffie suddenly
asked, looking round the room.

'Isn't he here?' I turned my head quickly
to look too.

'Maybe we left him downstairs,' Saffie
said.

'No, he was definitely here before.
She must have taken him.' My eyes were
pricking with tears as I remembered what
had happened to Granny's panda bear.

'But I don't understand. Why would Queenie-May *want* him?' Saffie asked, going over to the window again. She jumped back in shock as a shrill voice suddenly answered her from outside.

'*To make sure you don't tell any interfering grown-ups about me, of course!*'

And there was Queenie-May, her long dress hitched up and tucked into her knickers as she climbed back over the window ledge into the room.

'Queenie-May, where have you been? What have you done with Howard?' I demanded furiously, but she only smirked while busying herself with straightening out her dress.

'You shall have him back in due course if you are good little girls and don't tell anyone about me,' she finally said. 'Oh – and I want a ride in that fabulous aeroplane I just went to have a look at in your front garden.'

'That's impossible,' I said promptly. 'Grandpa's aeroplane can't fly. There's no engine.'

'Come now, Emma, that shouldn't be a problem for you girls, should it?' She gave me a knowing look. 'Anyway, Saffie's already told me she's planning to make it fly on your grandfather's birthday tomorrow.'

I looked at my sister. 'You are?'

Saffie flushed. 'I thought we could have a surprise midnight feast on Grandpa's birthday and that I could make his aeroplane fly over the garden with a banner saying HAPPY BIRTHDAY! I was *going* to tell you . . . I was just worried in case you said it wasn't a good idea.'

'Well, *I* think it's a marvellous idea!'

113

Queenie-May declared in her silkiest voice. 'Though you won't see the HAPPY BIRTHDAY banner in the dark of course. That's why I've volunteered to ride in the plane. That way I can shine a torch directly on it as we fly by!'

'No way,' I said at once, whirling round to face her. 'There's no way you're going anywhere near Grandpa's plane!'

'I beg your pardon?' Queenie-May narrowed her eyes, her tone of voice instantly becoming threatening. 'I'd start planning that midnight party *now* if I were you, Emma, and one way or another you *will* arrange that aeroplane ride for me. Unless of course you never want to see your precious teddy bear ever again!'

CHAPTER 8

The following day was Grandpa's birthday
and we woke up to discover that Granny
had sneaked into our room while we were
sleeping and taken Saffie's Supergirl outfit
to put in the wash. Lying on the bottom of
Saffie's bed was a pretty summer dress.

'Saffie, please don't make a big fuss,' I
begged when she looked really cross. 'We
don't want to spoil today for Grandpa. Mum
and Dad will be here soon, so let's just get
ready and go downstairs.' I went over to pull
back the curtains and take a look outside.

'It's a glorious day for a plane ride, don't you think?' Queenie-May greeted me cheerfully from her seat on the sunny window ledge. She had stayed there all night hidden from view behind the closed curtains. 'Perhaps it would be more fun to fly during the day? What do you think?'

'I think you're a very bad doll and if you don't tell us where Howard is you'll be sorry,' I threatened.

Queenie-May just laughed in my face and said she would tell us after we organized her plane ride.

Mum and Dad arrived later that morning (after Saffie and I had spent ages searching in vain for Howard). Our parents were gobsmacked when they saw Grandpa's model plane and Dad stayed out on the front lawn for ages, admiring it and asking Grandpa loads of questions.

As soon as Mum came inside I grabbed her hand and took her straight into the living room to show her the doll's house.

'Oooh!' she burst out when she saw it on the coffee table. 'I haven't seen that for years!'

'Come and look inside,' I said, opening up the front for her and making the most of having her all to myself since Saffie had stayed outside with Dad and Grandpa.

'Oh, Emma, this is marvellous!' she said, kneeling down next to me to get a closer look. 'I'd forgotten how cute the furniture was – look at the teeny fish tank! Oh, and isn't the little rocking horse sweet? Oh, look. There's Mrs Percival, the nanny – I'd forgotten how stern she was! And there are Clancy and Lucy, the twins.'

When I asked Mum if it would spoil it for her if I made the dolls come alive she gave me a funny look, so I quickly explained what Grandpa had told me.

She laughed. 'Oh, yes! I remember now. I told Granny that *I* wanted to be in charge of my doll's house, not her! I was a stubborn little thing back then, always wanting to do everything on my own! But actually I think it would be great fun if you brought the dolls to life for us, Emma!'

So I did, and it *was* really good fun getting to know the doll's-house family together. (Though Mrs Percival gave Mum quite a telling-off for scaring the children when she first stuck her head inside the nursery to say hello!)

★

'So *now* what do you think the chances are of Saffie being able to go to school after the summer?' I heard Mum asking Granny later as they made lunch.

Saffie was out in the back garden playing, and I had come into the kitchen to get a drink.

Granny laughed. 'About zero!'

Mum sighed. 'Has she been really awful?'

'Ever since I had to confiscate Elvira and Dorothy she's been difficult. Mind you, Emma's come on a lot. She's much more confident about using her superpower now.'

Mum sighed again. 'Mother, you do realize I sent the girls here hoping that Saffie would learn to use her power *less* – not so that Emma could learn to use hers *more*.'

'But, Mum, we have to learn to use our powers properly so that we can take care of ourselves,' I pointed out.

'Really?' Mum gave me an unimpressed look and I could tell she thought I was just quoting Granny. 'In case you haven't noticed, you and Saffie are still children, which means you don't *have* to take care of yourselves. That's what I'm here for. And Daddy.'

'Yes, but—'

'Actually there are no buts,' she interrupted me. 'You see, *I* think there's a reason why this superpower always skips a generation. *I* think it's because those in the family who have it need the protection of their parents – and later on their children – who don't.'

None of us spoke for a moment or two and I looked at Granny to see if she was going to comment.

Finally Granny said, 'That's an interesting point, Marsha, especially if you think about what happened to your Aunt Penelope. Perhaps having a family of her own might have made a difference . . .'

'Perhaps,' Mum agreed, 'though we'll never know for sure. Anyway . . . let's not think about Aunt Penelope now. Come on . . . We'd better tell Dad about the birthday treat we've got planned for him today. We thought you could come too, Mother, and Jim can stay here with the girls.'

It turned out that Mum was planning to take Grandpa to a huge model aeroplane exhibition that afternoon.

'Can't we come too?' Saffie and I both begged when we first heard about it.

Mum explained that this was an exhibition for grown-up collectors and that there would be lots of different model aeroplanes and lots and lots of information posted up about each one of them, all of which Grandpa would want to read carefully.

'I'm sure you'd both get very bored,' she said firmly. 'I really think you'll be better off staying here with Daddy. If you ask him nicely I'm sure he'll take you to the park.'

'The *park*? Oh *yes*, I really want to go to the park!' my sister exclaimed at once, and I knew right away what she was thinking. The play park near Granny's house has a massive climbing frame that both Granny and Mum are too scared to let Saffie go on. Dad would let her play on it though.

'Mum, is it all right if we give Grandpa his birthday present at his party?' I asked after Grandpa had gone upstairs to get ready for his afternoon out. (We'd already asked Granny if we could throw Grandpa a surprise midnight feast and she'd thought it a brilliant idea.)

'Of course,' Mum said, giving me a smile.

'We're going to make Grandpa a birthday jelly too, after you've gone,' Saffie added with a grin. 'But don't worry – he doesn't actually have to eat it!'

We had just made the jelly, which I was putting in the fridge to set, when Dad got a phone call from his work. Dad always says he'll just be a minute when he answers work calls – but it nearly always takes much longer.

I went to join Saffie in the front garden and found her looking a bit alarmed as she stood staring at Grandpa's model plane. I soon saw why. Queenie-May was sitting in the cockpit, a bright red headscarf tied around her hair and my sister's swimming goggles covering her eyes. I had to admit that she was such a good fit she could almost have been the real model pilot.

'What are you doing here?' I hissed.

'I am waiting for my aeroplane ride,' Queenie-May replied haughtily. 'Though it would have been nice if you'd had the decency to come and fetch me. It's extremely difficult climbing down that ivy in this gown. By the way, Saffie, it's so pleasing to see *you* in a pretty dress for a change – much more appropriate than that ridiculous fancy-dress costume!'

Saffie gave Queenie-May a furious glare. 'My Supergirl outfit is *not* ridiculous!'

Queenie-May laughed. 'Do you know,

you remind me of that other little girl
I lived with! Penelope had the dearest,
crossest scowl, just like you, and she had a
wonderfully bad temper. She and I got into
so much trouble together! It was such fun! I
can teach you some of the naughty tricks we
used to play on people if you like.'

'I don't need *you* to teach me anything!'
my sister replied sharply.

Queenie-May just laughed again. 'Do
you know, I'm getting to like you more and
more the crosser you get? I always did prefer
strong-willed little girls. I'd much rather play
with *you* than Little Miss Boring over there.'

'My sister is *not* boring,' Saffie defended
me. 'She's *sensible* – and she can't even help
that because Mummy says she was born that
way.'

'Saffie—' I began, not sure whether to be

125

annoyed because she was making it sound like I had something wrong with me, or pleased because she was standing up for me to Queenie-May.

'Look – are you going to bring this plane to life or not?' Queenie-May goaded her. 'Because the sooner you do, the sooner I'll tell you where I left that rotten old bear.'

'You'd *better* tell!' Saffie snarled back. She saw Queenie-May's darkening expression and quickly gave in. 'I can get the plane to fly you over those woods and back. Will that do?'

'That sounds perfect,' Queenie-May replied with a triumphant grin.

'Saffie . . . be careful . . .' I murmured, but even *I* was beginning to think this might be the only way to find Howard.

Saffie slid shut the cockpit roof and stood

back to focus all her attention on Grandpa's plane.

Pretty soon the plane was looking different. Saffie nearly always gives things faces when she animates them and this was no exception. The plane had grown a smiley mouth and two round eyes on stalks, and Queenie-May let out a shriek of delight as it started to move. First it rolled over the grass and then on to the driveway, rolling bumpily across the ground on its little wheels.

'Saffie, where's it going?' I asked as we followed it.

I nearly jumped out of my skin when the plane answered for itself. 'To find a runway, of course!'

The plane turned on to the pavement and started to pick up speed as I kept my fingers

crossed that no neighbours were looking.

I watched Saffie running after it shouting out instructions that I couldn't hear. Then she stood back and watched as it took off.

'Wow!' I gasped, only wishing that Grandpa could see his beautiful aeroplane soaring up into the sky so gracefully. Not for the first time I wished that I could animate very large objects like Saffie could.

I followed my sister as she hurried round
to the back of the house. She didn't take her
eyes off the plane as it flew over the field
behind the house, and on over the woods,
getting smaller and smaller the further away
it got.

Suddenly the plane tipped over abruptly
so that it was flying upside down.

'I hope *that's* exciting enough for her,'
Saffie said through gritted teeth.

Before it could disappear from view the plane turned round in a little arc and began to fly back over the woods – the right way up this time.

Just then Dad appeared in the kitchen doorway holding our bowl of jelly. 'Girls, I think you've put too much water in this. It doesn't look like it's going to set.' He looked up and let out a startled gasp as he spotted Grandpa's plane – and the bowl of jelly slipped through his fingers.

As the glass bowl smashed on to the concrete patio Saffie's concentration broke.

'Saffie!' I cried out, but it was too late.

All we could do was watch in horror as Grandpa's aeroplane nosedived into the trees.

CHAPTER 9

'What are we going to do?' I murmured, almost in tears after my sister had tried to re-animate the plane by imagining it in her head and found that she couldn't.

Dad was furious with us. 'How could you do this to Grandpa?' he yelled. It was hard to have him looking at us like we were criminals.

'Let's bring the gnomes to life,' Saffie suggested suddenly.

Dad looked at her as if he thought she had gone completely loopy. 'Why?' he demanded.

'Because we need a search-and-rescue team,' Saffie reasoned. 'That's what would happen if the plane was real.'

I thought about the time a bird had fallen down our grandparents' chimney and got stuck behind their blocked-up fireplace. The gnomes had carried out a brilliant rescue mission using some rope that had been in the garage, and one of them had abseiled down the inside of the chimney with a pen torch gripped between his teeth. (That was before Granny had bought them night-vision goggles.)

'It's amazing what Granny's gnomes can do when they work together, Daddy,' Saffie added.

'It's true, Dad,' I backed her up. 'Granny calls them her mini commandos.' And as I thought about that I started to get an idea.

132

'Shall I bring them all to life right now?' Saffie was saying enthusiastically.

As Dad pulled a horrified face I said quickly, 'Wait a minute, Saffie. I don't think we need to.'

And I slowly outlined my plan.

'So you want to fly *one* of the gnomes over the accident site to look for the plane – a sort of reconnaissance mission if you like?' Dad clarified slowly. 'And you want to send this gnome there on the back of one of the topiary birds from your grandmother's hedge?'

I nodded. 'We *could* just send the bird on its own, but I think that a gnome's feedback might be more reliable. So will you cut one of the birds off the hedge for us, Dad?'

Dad sighed. 'Do I have a choice?'

133

'Let's use the seagull, Daddy,' Saffie suggested. 'It already has its wings spread out as if it's flying, so I won't have to make it grow them. It will be easy to fly as it is.'

As Dad went to the garage to fetch Grandpa's hedge-cutter, Saffie and I discussed which gnome would be the best one to animate.

'I think we should ask Walter what he thinks,' Saffie said as Dad came back and set to work on the hedge.

'No way,' I replied. 'He'll want to know what happened and he won't stop lecturing us for ages.'

The hedge seagull was quite jumpy once Saffie had brought her to life. 'A plane crash in the trees you say?' she squawked. 'Are any nests destroyed? Are any trees on fire? I don't want my feathers singed!'

'You're
not *made* of
feathers –
you're made of
leaves,' I pointed
out, but the highly
strung bird just gave me a panicky stare with
the beady eyes Saffie had given her.

Saffie and I eventually agreed that the best
gnome for the job was the one who had
rescued the bird from Granny's chimney,
since he was obviously brave and didn't
mind heights. His name was Percy and he
was Granny's accordion-playing gnome. He
wore bright orange dungarees, which meant
he was very easy to spot.

As soon as Percy was animated and
we had explained what we needed him
to do he put down his accordion and

began some warm-up stretches.

'I always like to limber up before a mission,' he explained before throwing himself down on the ground to do some press-ups.

Keeping a safe distance away, Dad cleared his throat to get our attention. 'Emma, do you think you could tell . . . um . . . Percy to be very careful not to accidently dislodge the plane if it *is* stuck in the trees?'

'Don't you worry, Jim,' Percy answered him directly. 'I know exactly what I'm doing!'

Poor Dad turned pale and I had a feeling he found it really disturbing to be on first-name terms with a garden gnome.

Nobody spoke while Percy and the seagull were away, though we all started speaking at once the second they landed safely on the back lawn again.

'It's good news! The plane *is* caught in the treetops,' Percy informed us with a grin as he jumped off on to the ground.

'What about the doll?' I asked. 'Is she all right?'

'I think so. She's certainly still on board. I want to fly back there now with a couple of ropes. I can throw down the ends of the ropes to that doll and get her to tie them on. Then it should be possible to tow the whole thing out of the trees. But we have to hurry. It looks as if it could fall at any minute.'

'Dad, can you please go and see if there's any rope in the garage?' I said urgently.

'I'll be as quick as I can,' Dad replied.

He soon arrived back from the garage with two coils of rope, which he and Percy

carefully tied around the seagull's middle.
He looked nervous as he asked, 'So what
will we say if the neighbours see any of this?'

'We say we're flying some remote-
controlled toys,' I answered straight away.
'But don't worry, Dad. Granny and
Grandpa's neighbours aren't nosy like ours.'

'OK,' Percy said in a taking-charge sort of
voice. 'Let's do this. Saffie, are you ready?'

And my little sister looked very serious as
she nodded that she was.

We had to struggle to stay calm as we
watched the hedge seagull fly away with
Percy on board. Saffie kept her gaze
focused on the bird while Dad and I
stood beside her. I was animating Percy
this time. The bird flew as far as the
trees and stopped, hovering there while

Percy lowered the ropes down.

I felt really nervous about what would happen next. Would Queenie-May be able to tie on the ropes? Would they hold? How precariously balanced was the plane? Had it been damaged in the crash?

The hedge bird was flapping its green leafy wings furiously, hovering high above the trees as it waited for the signal from Percy to pull out the stranded plane.

'There it is!' I exclaimed excitedly as the plane suddenly emerged from the trees.

As soon as she saw it my sister started clutching her tummy, which she always does when she's animating something very difficult. I really wished I could help, but since I'd never been able to move large objects I knew it would be too risky to start trying now. Soon Saffie was red in the face

139

from the effort of animating both the bird and the plane from such a long distance away.

'Where are they going to land?' Dad muttered as they got slowly closer, still connected by the ropes as they flew side by side. 'The garden isn't going to be much of a landing strip for the plane.'

Then we saw that Percy was untying the ropes from around the hedge bird. With the ropes no longer holding the two together the plane began to descend, clearly planning to use the field behind the house as a runway, while the bird with Percy on board continued to fly towards the house.

The plane made a very bumpy landing in the field. As soon as it was on the ground Saffie withdrew her power and she did the same to the hedge bird as soon as it had landed. Percy remained very much alive and I felt as if keeping him that way was getting so easy that it was even possible to do it without focusing all my attention on him.

'Come on,' Dad said, heading at once for the field. 'Let's go and inspect the damage.'

'Saffie, are you OK?' I asked, hardly able to believe that my sister had concentrated for so long.

She was no longer clutching her tummy as she smiled up at me and nodded.

'Come on then,' I said, helping her up. 'We don't want to leave poor Dad alone for too long with Queenie–May, do we?'

CHAPTER 10

By the time Mum got home with Granny and Grandpa late that afternoon, Dad had repaired the plane's scratched paintwork as best he could and put it back in the garage to dry. But he was still furious with us.

Queenie-May had told him that the plane ride had been *our* idea and of course we couldn't go against her since we still didn't know where Howard was. Dad didn't know that Queenie-May was a special doll, so it was unlikely that he would bother mentioning her to Mum or Granny.

However, he had spent the rest of the afternoon struggling to decide whether to tell them about Grandpa's plane. In the end he decided to wait until the next day so that he didn't spoil Grandpa's birthday, and he even managed to temporarily fix the seagull back on top of the hedge.

Unfortunately Queenie-May wasn't so easy to fix. She must have hit her face on something in the crash, because several big cracks had appeared on one cheek. She had totally freaked out when she saw herself in the mirror and refused to tell us anything about Howard. 'You should be worrying about *me* – not that silly old bear!'

'Saffie . . . I think we should tell Granny about Queenie-May,' I said as soon as we were alone. 'Maybe she'll be able to help.'

'No! Then Queenie-May won't *ever* tell us where Howard is,' Saffie protested.

'Queenie-May isn't going to tell us in any case,' I said.

'But Granny will be really angry if she finds out. I don't *want* to tell her, Emma.' My sister was looking quite upset.

'Don't worry – if you like I'll tell her on my own,' I said.

I waited until later when Granny was on her own in the kitchen secretly putting the final touches to Grandpa's birthday cake, which we were going to have at our midnight feast that night. It was a double-layered vanilla sponge-cake with pink icing, strawberries and chocolate flakes on the top, and Granny had made a little aeroplane out of marzipan and stuck it in the middle.

'That looks yummy, Granny,' I said as she

finally stood back to inspect it.

'Wait until you see the birthday dessert Donald made. I've hidden it in the garage for now. I thought we could keep it for our midnight party too.'

Donald had dropped by half an hour earlier with a birthday card and a present for Grandpa. I hadn't realized he'd brought a dessert as well.

'It's a shame Donald can't come to Grandpa's party, isn't it?' I said.

'Don't worry. We'll save him a nice big piece of birthday cake,' Granny promised.

Mum and Dad and Saffie were all in the living room keeping Grandpa distracted while Granny saw to the cake, so I reckoned now would be a good time to tell Granny about Queenie-May without any interruptions. But first I had a question to ask.

'Granny, I've been thinking . . .' I began cautiously. 'Do you know *why* Queenie-May is so powerful that she can't be de-animated?'

Granny looked across at me with a bit of a twinkle in her eye. 'You certainly are interested in that old doll, aren't you? All right then, I'll tell you . . . though I warn you, it's rather an incredible story. You see, when my sister and I were children, Penelope decided we should *both* try and animate Queenie-May at exactly the same time. We'd been told by our grandmother that dual animation was impossible – that one of us would always make the connection with the doll a split second before the other. Penelope wanted to prove

146

our grandmother wrong – she always liked proving grown-ups wrong – and she became quite obsessed with it. So we tried over and over for a very long time and one day . . . well . . . it actually *worked*. It must have been a complete fluke, because we certainly never managed it again. But it left Queenie-May with double the animation power inside her and when we tried to de-animate her after that we found we couldn't. Unless she allowed it.

To start with she would let us de-animate her if we bribed her with a promise of a present or some other treat. She loved new clothes and being taken with us on days out. But gradually it became harder and harder to find something to tempt her with and it got more and more difficult to get her to let us switch her off. And then there was that awful day on the pier and, well . . . you know the rest . . .'

'Yes,' I said. 'Wow . . .' It really was quite a story.

'I suppose I'd better come and deal with her, hadn't I?' Granny said.

'Deal with who?' I asked in surprise.

'Queenie-May, of course! I know Saffie found her and brought her to life. I overheard the two of them talking to each other in your room.'

'Really?' I was astonished.

'I was going to jump in and confiscate her straight away, but then I thought it might be good for Saffie to have to face the consequences of her actions for once. So I decided to let her – and you – get on with it. I did wonder how long you would wait before you finally came to me for help.'

'Oh, Granny, I'm sorry,' I gushed, feeling guilty and relieved both at the same time.

'Come on. Let's go and speak to Queenie-May, shall we? I'm guessing she's been giving you a hard time. You'd better start by telling me everything she's done.' As we went upstairs together I told Granny about Howard, which didn't seem to surprise her in the least. But when I told her about the accident with Grandpa's plane, she nearly had a fit and I had the feeling she was struggling not to lose her temper with me.

In our bedroom Queenie-May was lying on Saffie's bed with her eyes closed, looking very sorry for herself. When she heard us come in, she opened her eyes, then started to laugh. '*Harriet*, is that really you?'

I realized that Queenie-May probably

hadn't actually seen Granny since she was a girl.

'My but you're *old*,' Queenie-May continued. 'Really, *really* old. Your skin is so wrinkly I wouldn't have recognized you if it wasn't for your eyes, and even they've got big bags underneath them. But then Penelope always was the pretty one!'

'Talking of faces . . .' Granny replied with a glare, '*you* seem to have injured yours rather badly.'

Queenie-May immediately put a protective hand up to her injured cheek. 'Indeed I have, thanks to your hopeless granddaughter, who can't even keep a model plane up in the air.'

'You brought this on yourself, Queenie-May,' Granny told her sternly. 'Luckily I know a doll restorer who does very fine work on antique dolls like you, but if I arrange for your face to be repaired you have to give us something in return. You have to tell us *at once* where Howard is.'

Queenie-May snorted. 'Don't tell me you're still worried about that useless old lump of scratchy fur! Well, I can tell you what happened to him if you want, but you're not going to like it!'

And she told us she had stuffed Howard into the passenger footwell of Grandpa's plane. 'He was there for the flight – though he didn't know anything about it of course. After we crashed into the trees I was terrified the plane was going to fall, so I decided I'd better try and lighten the load. After all, it's not as though Howard is a lightweight sort of bear. I imagine he fell straight to the ground, being the dense lump that he is!'

'How *could* you . . . ?' I was almost too appalled to speak.

Queenie-May looked amused as she said, 'Well, I did *warn* you that you wouldn't like it!'

CHAPTER 11

Granny said she wanted to talk to Queenie-May on her own for a bit, so I went downstairs to find Saffie.

My sister was in the kitchen with Dad, and both of them were licking their fingers after dipping them in the icing on Grandpa's birthday cake.

'Just tidying it up, Emma,' Dad said, giving me a wink as my little sister started to giggle.

'I thought you were meant to be distracting Grandpa,' I said.

'He's fallen asleep in his chair,' Dad informed me.

'Snoring away as usual!' Saffie added with another giggle.

She soon stopped giggling when I told her about Queenie-May's confession.

'Oh no, poor Howard! We have to go and rescue him right now!' she exclaimed, looking all set to put on her wellies and go marching off into the woods to search for him straight away.

'What's going on?' Mum asked as she joined us.

Saffie and I looked at each other nervously, not knowing what we should tell her.

Granny came downstairs then and Saffie and I found the matter being taken out of our hands as she recounted everything to our mum. By the time Granny had finished talking both Saffie and I were flushing as Mum gave us her most furious glare.

It was all too much for Saffie. Having Mum angry with her as well as hearing the terrible news about Howard seemed to tip her over the edge and she suddenly started to cry.

'Don't worry, Saffie. We can go and look for Howard in the woods tomorrow,' Mum said, her stern expression softening a little.

Dad was frowning. 'It will be a bit like looking for a needle in a haystack, won't it?'

Granny looked thoughtful. 'Not necessarily. Marsha, is your father still asleep in the other room?'

Mum nodded.

'Good! Henry would sleep all night in his armchair if I let him, so I doubt he'll wake up before the party.'

'Shouldn't we wake him up anyway to tell him about his aeroplane?' Mum asked.

'Goodness no! It's best if he doesn't know what happened to it until tomorrow or he'll spend the whole night in the garage checking it over for damage. Now . . . start putting up the decorations everyone, while I go and have a word with Walter about Emma's bear.'

While Granny spoke quietly with Walter, Dad put up the fairy lights in the garden and the rest of us blew up the balloons Granny had bought saying HAPPY 70th BIRTHDAY! Eventually Granny came to report back to us.

'It's just as I thought,' she said briskly. 'Walter *is* willing to organize a search party to look for Howard tonight. But they'll need our help, so listen carefully while I tell you what we have to do . . .'

'This *could* work I suppose,' Mum murmured as we stood in the back garden half an hour later watching Granny's gnomes being flown towards the woods. 'Though I think it's a bit of a long shot.'

'Aren't all your mother's crazy ideas?' Dad whispered back.

Mum and Dad kept quiet after that as we watched Granny and Saffie at work. Granny was sitting on a deckchair in the garden, facing the woods. She had closed her eyes to concentrate better, totally absorbed in keeping all her gnomes animated now that they were tiny specks in the distance, huddled together on the backs of the two flying hedge birds. Saffie was sitting next to her, keeping the hedge birds animated – the duck had been recruited now along with the seagull – as they hovered above the wood.

The light was fading and it was difficult to see clearly, but we could make out two long ropes being dangled down into the trees. Then one by one we saw Granny's gnomes climbing down the ropes. They looked just like mini commandos being dropped into the jungle to carry out some top-secret mission.

'But will you be able to keep all the gnomes animated when you can't see any of them, Granny?' I had asked her uncertainly when she had first told us Walter's plan.

'Oh yes! I know my gnomes like the back of my hand, so don't worry about that,' Granny had said. 'But that brings me to *your* task, Emma. It would be helpful if Howard was animated too, so that he can call out to attract the search party's attention . . .'

And so I had promised Granny that I would take on the task of bringing Howard to life.

'Are you OK, Emma?' Mum whispered now as I prepared myself to begin.

I nodded, though in fact I was still scared that I wouldn't be able to do this.

'Just do your best,' Mum said. 'That's all Granny wants.'

I closed my eyes and tried to picture Howard in my mind just as I'd done when Granny was teaching me 'blind' animation before. It was harder now though, because he was so much further away. Then with enormous relief I felt the 'ping' inside my head that I was sure meant he had come to life wherever he was. I just hoped I could keep him that way for long enough and that he wasn't too frightened. And above all else I hoped that the gnomes would find him.

Eventually, after what seemed like forever (although in fact it was no more than half an hour), my concentration began to wane and I suddenly felt the sort of releasing feeling inside my head that happens when an animation is over. I was almost too exhausted to speak and my head was pounding so hard I felt like it might explode.

Mum said, 'I think you should go to bed now, Emma.'

'What time is it?' I croaked.

'Nine o'clock. The hedge birds aren't needed any longer so Saffie has already gone.'

I realized then that my sister wasn't in the garden with us. I hadn't even been aware of her going upstairs. Granny was still sitting in her deckchair with her eyes closed and her brow furrowed in concentration.

'What about Grandpa?' I asked.

'He was still asleep in his chair the last time I looked,' Dad said. 'Come on. I'll take you to bed. Don't worry, we'll wake you up for the party.'

★

At a quarter to midnight Saffie's alarm clock rang out. She must have set it before she went to sleep.

'Turn it off, Saffie,' I mumbled groggily, putting my hands over my ears.

As she jumped out of bed I saw she was back in her Supergirl outfit, newly washed and ironed by Granny. 'I wonder if the gnomes are back yet,' she said enthusiastically as she turned off the alarm.

That thought made me wake up properly too. 'Wait for me,' I called out as I climbed out of bed to go with her. At least Queenie-May wasn't in our room any more. (Granny had decided to move the doll to *her* room to keep her away from Saffie.)

Mum and Dad were in the kitchen sipping mugs of tea and murmuring to each other when we got downstairs.

'What are you two doing up?' Mum asked when she saw us.

'Saffie set her alarm for the midnight feast,' I explained. 'But why didn't you wake us?' As I spoke, I looked out of the window and saw that Granny was *still* sitting in the garden. 'Aren't they back yet?' I asked in surprise.

Mum shook her head, looking worried.

'That's why I think you should go back to bed. I don't think tonight is the right time to have a party.'

Saffie scowled. 'But it's Grandpa's birthday *today*! It won't *be* a birthday party if we don't do it now! And we've still got his special present to give him and his birthday cake!'

I was just about to ask Mum what the special present was, as we still didn't know, when we heard a noise outside. Granny was standing up and making her way to the open gate at the bottom of the garden. The moon was half hidden behind a cloud, but there was just enough light for us to make out the group of small figures shuffling through it.

'Where's Howard?' I murmured. Then I saw that the gnomes were carrying a small stretcher between them. 'Oh!' I rushed out into the garden.

The gnome rescue party had placed a homemade stretcher – which was made from twigs and leaves cleverly woven together – down on the grass. Howard was laid out on top of it.

'Is he all right?' I asked anxiously, going to pick him up. Even though he wasn't animated I still wanted to give him a hug.

'He seems to be,' Percy told me. 'It took us a while to find him though. He was stuck in a tree branch and we couldn't see him from the ground. In fact we'd probably *never* have found him if we hadn't heard him shouting for all he was worth. Cedric and I had to climb up the tree to help him down.'

Granny looked exhausted, but even so she was beaming at me. 'See, Emma. They wouldn't have found Howard at all if it hadn't been for you.'

'Yes,' said Mum with a smile. 'Well done, Emma!'

Dad gave me a wink.

Suddenly a gruff sleepy voice from behind us asked, 'What's going on out here?' and we all turned to see Grandpa standing at the back door gazing at us. He looked bewildered as he took in the fairy lights and the balloons decorating the garden.

Saffie responded before the rest of us had a chance. 'This is your surprise birthday party, Grandpa! And you don't need to feel shy, because the only people coming to it will be *us*!'

CHAPTER 12

'I do believe this is the best birthday party I've ever been to,' Grandpa declared with a smile as we all gathered around the kitchen table where Granny had lit the candles on his cake.

As we sang 'Happy Birthday To You', Howard sang louder than anyone in his deep growly voice and I suddenly felt so lucky to have him back again that I felt a big lump in my throat. Walter and Cedric and Percy were there too – Granny seemed able to animate all three with no trouble now that they were in the same room as her.

Granny had put seven candles on the top of Grandpa's cake – one for every ten years of his life. Since seven was also the number Saffie was going to be on *her* next birthday, Grandpa insisted she help him blow them out to 'get in some practice'.

Afterwards we all clapped, then Mum left the room and came back with Grandpa's birthday present.

'I don't believe it!' Grandpa exclaimed after he had undone the very large parcel.

'What is it?' Saffie wanted to know.

'It's an engine . . . *the* engine for my aeroplane . . .' He sounded absolutely overwhelmed as he added, 'But this is too much . . . you really shouldn't have . . .' And his eyes filled up with tears.

'We wanted to, Dad,' Mum said, giving his arm a rub.

'Just make sure you don't crash the thing the first time you fly it, OK?' Dad joked, giving Saffie a secret wink.

Grandpa chuckled. 'I might have to get some lessons from Donald first.' Suddenly he looked puzzled. 'But wait a minute . . .

If you bought me this engine then you must have already known what I was making in there.' He looked at Granny. 'I don't understand. Donald was the only one I told. It was meant to be a big surprise for the rest of you.'

'I know,' Granny said. 'I'm sorry, dear. You left the garage unlocked one day and I couldn't resist having a little peep. There wasn't much to see at that stage – just the frame really – but afterwards I spoke to Donald about it, and then Marsha and Jim and I decided to give you a rather special birthday surprise.'

Grandpa looked stunned. 'But the other day when I showed it to you, you seemed . . . well . . .'

'Shocked and amazed?' Granny said. 'That's because I was! I never dreamed it would turn out like it has.'

Grandpa looked at us all before slowly beginning to laugh. 'Well in any case, thank you all very much. It's a wonderful birthday gift.'

'I don't understand,' Saffie whispered to me as we watched Grandpa carefully reading the instruction booklet that came with the engine. 'Granny can make his plane fly for him whenever he wants. Why does he need an engine?'

I remembered what Grandpa had said about how Mum had never liked Granny using her superpower to animate the people in her doll's house.

'It wouldn't be the same if Granny did it,' I said. 'Grandpa wants to make it fly *himself.*'

'Oh,' Saffie said in surprise. And she went

quiet as if she was thinking about that for the first time.

'Everyone, may I have your attention, please?' Granny suddenly announced, and we looked up to see her standing in the doorway holding a big plate.

'Is that what I think it is?' I murmured to Saffie as Granny walked into the room with a big grin on her face. On the plate was a large green jelly slug.

'Donald made this especially for you, Henry!' Granny told him.

The green slug-shaped jelly had two small jelly sweets as eyes stuck on the top of two chocolate fingers, which were protruding from its head in place of feelers.

Grandpa started laughing straight away. 'I don't believe it . . .'

'Don't tell me Donald found a slug-shaped jelly mould!' Mum exclaimed in disbelief.

'Apparently so!' Granny smiled at Grandpa. 'Don't worry, dear. We won't make you eat it! But you do have to have your photo taken with it to send to your brother!'

'After that can I eat it?' Saffie asked. 'I *love* slug jelly!'

And that made us all start giggling.

174

★

'Marsha, I need to talk to you about the rest of the summer,' Granny said the following day as Mum and I were with her in the kitchen.

Mum instantly looked worried and I could tell she was afraid Granny wanted to send us home right now.

'The thing is,' Granny continued, 'I'd like you to stay here for the summer too, Marsha. I think you might be right about the girls being too much for me to handle on my own. Besides, I think *they*'d prefer it if you were here.'

'Oh, yes, Mum, we would,' I said at once. 'Please stay!'

'Of course I'll stay,' Mum replied, sounding relieved. 'You don't have to persuade me – you know that's what I wanted in the first place.'

'Good, then that's settled.' Granny paused. 'You know, Marsha, Saffie did very well last night. She didn't have a single lapse in concentration managing those animated birds.'

'I know,' Mum agreed with a small smile. 'I guess there's definitely hope!'

Just then we heard a shout from upstairs.

'That sounds like Dad,' I said, and Mum and I left Granny and rushed upstairs to find out what was going on.

Saffie was already on the landing trying to calm down our dad, who looked like he'd just had the most terrible fright. 'Take deep breaths, Daddy . . . that's it . . .' she was saying.

'Jim, what happened? Are you all right?' Mum asked in concern.

'Why don't *you* tell them, Saffie?' Dad rasped, glowering at my sister, whose face immediately turned pink.

'I . . . Mummy, I *really* need to use the toilet,' Saffie blurted as she quickly escaped into the bathroom.

'Yes – and next time you can just knock on the door and *tell* me that!' Dad called out after her.

'Jim, what happened?' Mum asked again.

'Saffie happened – that's what,' Dad grunted. 'I know it was her because I heard her giggling outside . . .'

Dad told us how he had been in the bathroom, quietly sitting on the toilet reading a magazine, when suddenly two hideous eyes on stalks had popped out from the page in front of him. At the same time a pink papery tongue had shot out and started

177

scolding him about how long he was taking.

Before Mum or I could respond, a delighted giggle sounded from behind us. 'I believe that's what's known as a tongue lashing,' declared a familiar voice, and we turned to see Queenie-May standing watching us from the doorway of Granny's bedroom.

'Don't be too cross with Saffie,' the doll continued, looking amused. 'It was my idea. Penelope and I once tried a similar thing with *her* father – though that time we made the actual *lavatory* come alive.' She giggled again.

Mum seemed to find her voice. 'I don't care whose idea it was. Saffie should know better!' she said sharply.

Just then my little sister came out of the bathroom. 'I'm really sorry I scared you,

Daddy,' she said solemnly before turning to Queenie-May. 'OK, I've done what you wanted. Now *you* have to keep *your* promise.'

'Saffie, what are you talking about?' I asked, but my sister didn't reply.

Queenie-May sighed and gave Saffie a little nod. 'All right. I'm ready.'

At that Saffie scrunched up her brow and stared really hard at Queenie-May and in an instant the doll had become lifeless again.

'Saffie, how did you—' I began in disbelief.

'I went to see her in Granny's room this morning,' Saffie explained. 'I said she'd have to let me de-animate her sooner or later if she wanted to get her face mended. She told me she knew that but she didn't want it to happen before she'd had any fun. So I said we could do something *really* fun together this morning if she agreed to let me de-animate her afterwards.'

'And that was all it took to persuade her?' Mum sounded incredulous.

'Yes . . . well, that and promising to bring her to life again the next time we come to Granny's!'

'Saffie—' Mum began hotly, but fortunately Dad intervened.

'So, Saffie,' he said swiftly, 'are you saying that the real reason you played that horrible trick on me was because Queenie-May suggested it in exchange for letting you de-animate her?'

My sister turned to Dad and nodded.

The corners of Dad's mouth twitched just a little. 'Hmm . . . well, I suppose that's a *bit* better than you being desperate for a wee and unable to just tell me that like any normal person.'

'Jim . . .' Mum began, and I could tell from her face that she was about to get started on how she didn't want Dad encouraging Saffie and me to think we weren't *normal*.

'Mum, it's OK,' I cut in quickly. 'Saffie and I *know* we're not normal, don't we, Saffie?'

181

My little sister nodded.

Mum looked crossly at both of us. 'Nonsense! You don't know what you're saying.'

'Yes we do!' I burst out impatiently. 'We have *superpowers*, Mum! So how can we be *normal*?'

Mum looked shocked and Dad was looking pretty surprised too.

'We're cool with it, Mum,' I added firmly. 'OK?'

'That's right, Mummy. We're cool with it,' Saffie echoed me solemnly.

'Oh . . .' And finally Mum's eyes teared up and she cracked a small smile as she held out her arms for Saffie and me to come to her for a hug.

Dad was smiling too as he came and put his arms around all three of us. 'There you

182

go, Marsha! They know they're not normal, but they're cool with it! Now how super is *that*?'

To read an exciting chapter,
please turn the page . . .

CHAPTER 1

My name is Emma, and I live with my perfectly ordinary mum Marsha, my perfectly ordinary dad Jim and my six-year-old sister Saffie.

Saffie and I both *look* ordinary enough – though if you met us you probably wouldn't guess that we're sisters. I have straight dark brown hair with brown eyes, whereas Saffie has extremely curly reddish-brown hair and blue eyes. I'm tall for my age, whereas Saffie is short for hers. I'm quite shy with people I don't know very well, whereas Saffie will chatter away to anyone.

But despite being different in many ways, we do have one very important thing in common . . .

You see we both have the same superpower!

It's not that Saffie and I can fly, or make ourselves invisible, or read minds, or make our bodies incredibly elastic or anything amazing like that. But what we *can* do is make all sorts of non-living objects come to life – which Mum says is called *animation*. This weird gift runs through my mum's side of the family but it always skips a generation, which is why it missed out Mum and jumped straight from Granny to us.

So now you're probably thinking, Wow! Having a superpower must be really cool! Well, it is in lots of ways . . . I mean, Saffie and I can do loads of extraordinary things that our friends can't. For instance, Saffie can make her dolls *really* talk to her – not

just pretend talking. And I can make my
pencils dance all over the desk if I get
bored while I'm doing my homework. And
we can have lots of fun with all Granny's
garden gnomes!

But it isn't all fun and games. Dad is
totally freaked out by our 'unnatural ability',
as he calls it. It gets a bit irritating after a
while, the way he just can't seem to get

used to the idea. I mean, he *still* nearly jumps out of his skin every time one of his shoes says hello to him when he goes to put it on. And then there's Mum, who you'd think would be pretty cool about the whole thing, wouldn't you? After all, she grew up in a house where the vacuum cleaner did the cleaning all on its own, the washing always hung itself out on the line to dry, and her toothbrush used to come and find her if she forgot to brush her teeth. But Mum says she hated having to live side by side with all those crazy objects that Granny had brought alive, especially as she had no control over them herself.

So anyway, Mum is just as stressed about our special powers as Dad is, and not just because she doesn't want to have to share her house all over again with a bunch of dancing brooms and out-of-control cutlery. She's also scared because she says that some people out there might want to take Saffie and me away and do lots of clever scientific tests on us if they find out about our powers.

Granny is always telling Mum to stop worrying so much. 'After all, nobody has turned them over to the local science laboratory yet, have they? And it isn't as if your neighbours haven't *already* witnessed a few odd things . . .'

Mum had to admit that Granny was right. You see, although Saffie and I are absolutely *not* allowed to use our superpowers outside the house, there are times when it just sort of happens – especially when Saffie is upset about something.

But then something changed that meant

8

even Granny had to agree that we totally *should* start worrying . . .

It was a Saturday at the start of the summer holidays when our new next-door neighbours moved in.

That afternoon Mum sat Saffie and me down together and spoke to us very solemnly. 'I want you two to be very careful around our new neighbours. We don't know what they're like, and remember . . . when it comes to your special ability, we can't trust *anybody*.'

'Yes, Mum . . . I know . . .' I said with a yawn, because, like I said before, our mother stresses all the time about other people finding out about us.

Saffie looked like she was hardly even listening. Her best friend, Rosie, had lived next door, and Saffie was so upset and cross about her moving away that she'd refused to say a proper goodbye or to stand outside and wave nicely with Mum and me as they'd driven off.

As soon as Mum had finished talking to us my sister muttered, 'Don't *care* about the new neighbours!' in a silly baby voice. Then she stomped upstairs and shut herself in her bedroom, where she started to play a very angry game with her dolls. It sounded as if they were calling each other names and throwing things at each other. It's weird, but it seems that when Saffie's in a bad mood everything she animates is in a bad mood too.

'Oh dear. I suppose we'd better check nothing's getting damaged up there,' Mum said with a sigh. I knew before she even said it what was coming next. 'You go, Emma. You're always so good with the dolls. If I go up there I'll lose my temper with them and it will only make things worse.'

I let out a big sigh too and put on my grumpiest face. 'Oh, Mum, do I *have* to?'

Mum got firm with me then and called me by my proper name, which I hate. 'Yes, Emmeline, you do. As I've told you many times before you are the best equipped to deal with your sister when she gets like this. I wish that wasn't the case, but it is. So please just go up there and see what you can do! And don't let that red-haired rag doll get the better of you – she's always the troublemaker!'

I trudged up the stairs, feeling cross.

'Serafina, what are you *doing*?' I demanded angrily as I pushed open her bedroom door. If Mum was going to call *me* by my proper name then I didn't see why I shouldn't call Saffie by *hers*. (Too late I remembered that lately my sister had started to absolutely love her name because she thinks it makes her sound like a very exotic princess.)

My sister didn't reply.

Inside her bedroom her two favourite dolls, Dorothy and Elvira, were squabbling with each other. Dorothy is a very cheeky-looking rag doll with brown freckles and long red woollen hair, and Elvira is an old hand-me-down dolly that was our mum's when she was a girl. Elvira has a soft lumpy body and a delicate china head, and Mum is always really protective of her. If you ask me, that's why Mum is so bad at handling any fights between Saffie's dolls, because she

always takes Elvira's side no matter what.

Elvira was the first object Saffie ever brought to life after Granny discovered a box of Mum's old toys in the loft when we were staying with her one time. Mum actually cried when Elvira stood up and smiled at her, partly because it was the first time Saffie had used her gift and partly because Mum suddenly remembered how much she had loved it when Granny had brought Elvira to life for her as a child. (She said she'd almost forgotten that there had been some *good* things about having a mum with a superpower.)

In Saffie's bedroom the floor around the two dolls was littered with smaller toys that had clearly been used as missiles. An entire dollies' tea-set was scattered about the room and there were books everywhere.

'I don't care if I never see you again, Miss *Straw-for-Brains*!' snapped Elvira rudely.

'My brains are made from the best quality stuffing!' Dorothy defended herself. 'And at least *my* head isn't hollow like yours. If your head ever gets cracked then we'll all be able to look inside and see that you haven't got any kind of brain at all!'

'Elvira! Dorothy!' I said sternly, but they ignored me.

Saffie was lying on her bed with a face like thunder. 'Go away!' she grunted at me without taking her eyes off the dolls.

I decided to try a different approach.

I chose the teddy bear that was sitting on Saffie's window ledge. His name is Howard and he's a sensible brown bear dressed in red dungarees and a little bow tie. Toys tend to have their own personalities (as well as being influenced by whoever brings them to life), and the more a toy gets animated then the stronger its personality becomes.

Howard used to be mine, which Mum says is the reason he's so level-headed. He's *always* sensible — even when Saffie threatens to de-animate him if he doesn't let his hair

15

down. In fact, once, when Saffie brought
him to life and gave him some rice to throw
down at Dad (who was mowing the lawn),
he told her she was very silly and actually
refused to do it.

I knew he was the perfect choice for
what I had in mind.

This is the bit that's difficult to describe –

what it actually feels like when you
make something come alive. All I can
say is that it doesn't hurt, it doesn't feel
unnatural, and when I was little I couldn't
understand why everyone else couldn't
do it too. It's really just a case of looking
at an object and then sort of mentally
zapping it into life. Of course the *zapping*
is the bit that's difficult to describe.
Granny says it uses a very special part of
our brains, a part that just doesn't function
that way in normal humans. (Dad calls it
the *wacky* part, though not in front of
Granny.)

As I focused really hard on Saffie's teddy
I felt that funny 'ping' inside my head, and
the next moment he was folding his arms
together and glaring severely at both dolls.
'Cut it out, both of you!' he growled in

a voice that made them jump. He stayed
standing on the window ledge as he
addressed Saffie sternly. 'Now just you listen
to me, young lady . . . We
all know how upset
you are about Rosie
moving away, but
she's only moved
to the other side
of town. You'll
still be able to see
her.'

Saffie looked
at me rather
than her teddy
as she replied,
'But we won't
be able to visit each other without a grown-
up and we won't be able to play in our

special den any more.' She and Rosie had converted the old garden shed in Rosie's garden into a den, and they used to spend hours playing there together.

I did feel sorry for her then because I knew how much she loved that den.

'Maybe the new family will have children too,' I said in an attempt to cheer her up. Rosie's mum hadn't known if they did or not – in fact she'd hardly known anything at all about the people who were buying her house. Dad says that's quite unusual. (Dad is an estate agent and he'd been a bit miffed that Rosie's parents hadn't asked *him* to sell their house so that he could personally vet our new neighbours.)

'I don't care if they *do* have children,' Saffie declared huffily.

'Well, you should. They might let you

play in their shed with them if you ask them nicely.'

'It's not up to them,' my sister said angrily. 'That shed is Rosie's and mine. It's our secret den and no one else is allowed inside unless *we* say so.'

'Don't be silly,' I said, starting to get impatient. 'Listen. The new people are moving in this afternoon. I'm going round to say hello to them later with Mum. Why don't you come too?'

But my little sister just narrowed her eyes and stubbornly shook her head. She can be very, *very* stubborn when she wants to be. 'I *told* Rosie I didn't want her to move away,' she declared, at which point Elvira lunged at Dorothy and gave her long woolly hair a sharp tug.

Dorothy yelped but immediately

recovered enough to grab a teacup to hurl at Elvira, who had climbed on to Saffie's beanbag chair, then up on to the window ledge to hide behind Howard. Just as Dorothy hurled the cup at her, Howard ducked and the cup hit Elvira smack in the face. Elvira started wailing and I rushed over to the window ledge to pick her up before Mum heard.

That's when I looked out of the window and spotted a boy my own age in the neighbouring garden, staring up at us. And judging by the look of disbelief on his face I was pretty sure he'd seen everything.

Gwyneth Rees

MY SUPER SISTER

Sometimes superpowers aren't so super ...

Being a big sister has never been so heroic!

Emma and her mischievous little sister Saffie like having superpowers — it's fun making your dolls come to life, teaching Dad's shoes to dance and playing frisbee with the garden gnomes. But it isn't always easy keeping their gift a secret — and when Saffie starts to use her powers in the naughtiest of ways, Emma has to think fast to save the day!

Gwyneth Rees

The Magic Princess Dress

**There are hundreds of beautiful dresses in every
colour of the rainbow — sewn with magic thread.
Take a look, try one on — and wait for the magic
to whisk you away on an amazing adventure!**

Ava is looking for her cat when she finds Marietta's
mysterious shop. She tries on a perfectly fitting gold and
emerald princess dress and whizzes through a secret
mirror — to fairytale land! Will she get there in time
to be a bridesmaid at Cinderella's wedding?

Gwyneth Rees

The Twinkling Tutu

There are hundreds of beautiful dresses in every colour of the rainbow — sewn with magic thread. Take a look, try one on — and wait for the magic to whisk you away on an amazing adventure!

Ava has just discovered the enchantment of Marietta's special dressing-up shop. Now she can't wait to try on a twinkling tutu with matching ballet slippers and pirouette back to Victorian times. Once there she finds she has an important part to play in making a girl's ballerina dreams come true!

There are hundreds of beautiful dresses in every colour of the rainbow — sewn with magic thread. Take a look, try one on — and wait for the magic to whisk you away on an amazing adventure!

When Ava puts on a sparkling trapeze outfit with a dazzling butterfly tiara, she is transported back in time to a travelling circus. Ava loves the clever circus stunts and the beautiful costumes, but she's worried about a baby elephant that is meant to perform tricks. Can Ava reunite the baby with its mother before the cruel animal trainer finds out?

There's a secret world at the bottom of the sea!

Rani came to Tingle Reef when she was a baby mermaid –
she was found fast asleep in a seashell, and nobody knows
where she came from.

Now strange things keep happening to her – almost as if
by magic. What's going on? Rani's pet sea horse, Roscoe,
Octavius the octopus and a scary sea-witch help her find
out . . .

Collect them all!